Bittersweet

Ann Holiday

Content Warning:

This book is filled with over the top holiday cheer. You know those predictable holiday movies where we already know the story but can't seem to stop watching each year? This is that book.. Happy holidays you ho ho hos and merry reading.

Dedication

May your cookies be sweet and your holiday be merry.

Chapter One

Five weeks until Christmas

The smell of warm vanilla wafted in plumes through the little bake shop on Frost Lane. Crushed candy canes and gumdrops littered the white quartz counters. Garlands of neatly iced gingerbread men, sparkling silver tinsel, and twinkling lights snared almost every surface. Casting a soft incandescent glow upon the bakery. The glass cases glittered with rows of sugared holiday-themed treats each one meticulously decorated. It was my own slice of holiday heaven. My sister Isla sat at one of the small cafe tables, well the only cafe table, her eyebrows furrowed deepening in concentration on her laptop. Isla often looked like that these days, always worried, always trying to prepare for the next disaster. I keep telling her I am going to get her botox for christmas but she doesn't seem to think it is as funny as I do. Her skin has taken a beating from being in the constant state of stress. I continued to watch her as my hands wrapped the braids of pink and green dough, folding in gumdrops within each nest I created. Against my better judgment I chucked a small purple one at Isla. Her furrowed eyebrows made the damn thing ricochet even harder. It bounced right off her head onto the table.

"You are a child!" She huffed curtly, not even bothering to look up.

The icy blonde hair that crowned her head was piled high in a claw clip. The folds of her nose crinkled as she tried to focus on whatever was on her screen. She always stressed to the max this time of year. If that was even possible. It was December 1st. Well, technically it was still November, it was just late as hell. We had stayed up most of the night changing out the decor and revamping the fall menu boards. Taking down any trace of autumn relics, replacing them with pumpkins with gingerbread, snowflakes and anything that glitters. The first day of December marked the official start date of all of the winter activities at the Bakery, which meant long hours of planning, baking, accounting, and my least favorite-cleaning. If magic was real that is what I would wish for. A self cleaning kitchen. No more scooping crusty batter out of the mixer or scrubbing caramel off dishes for me. It would be a sparkling paradise, that I could blow up with my baking mess. My sister has never learned to cope with the stress of this season, year after year she repeats herself. Trying to figure out what all town activities we were going to be included in and how we are going to budget and produce what we need. To me it seems like I do the same thing every year. We have had steady growth over the years with the town soaring in popularity. I have had to trial and error my number, but it always worked out in the end. Isla is an analyst. She has always wanted to know EXACTLY how much I was planning to make. The cost of the flour, the vanilla, the box, the stamp, yada yada yada. She has always been the brains, and I am the production. We are the only bakery in our charming little town so the mass influx of tourists each year is great for our business. It's just hard for me to keep up with demand alone after mom died.

Brushing my floured hands off I knew I needed more coffee to help fuel the rest of the night. Isla looked like she did too. My hands swayed over the coffee choices trying to decide what to make. We had just ordered some new espressos I was dying to try. I convinced Isla to grab some new syrups too. I had a fancy for these french coffee syrups and she could not convince me otherwise that anything else even tasted close to them. Surveying the glass bottles I went for my usual tonight, a white peppermint latte. I made us two steaming glasses without all the extra razzle dazzle that I give our customers. The ceramic santa mugs clinked against the table summoning Isla from her trance with her computer.

"Thank you, I needed this." She sipped from her mug. "You have always been able to make these perfectly. Just like mom." Her voice stuttered a little on her last few words.

We didn't talk about mom very often. The loss was still too painful for Isla. It was painful most days, especially here. Surrounded by every inch of a place that was filled with memories of her. My hand embraced hers gently, while summoning my warmest smile. Her finger squeezed back ever so slightly, easing the tension that filtrated the room. Sipping from my own cup I let the warm pepperminty-sweetness wash over me.

"This year is going to be the biggest yet, Hollie. They are projecting over 10,000 more tourists coming than they had last year. Especially since the new snow hill center is finished." I swear I could practically see her hair turning gray as she rattled off stats to me. How in the world our tiny town would fit that many people was a frightening thing to think of.

"You know I can handle it, I always have." I told her crossing my arms over my chest. She acted like I didn't solely bake at the production level of a little Debbie factory here.

"I'm not saying you can't, I just think... it might be good if you had help this year, we both know I cannot bake. I would burn the place down." Her arms raised to store around us. Her too big blue snowflake crew neck slouched down her arms.

"You know how I feel about that. I hate to relinquish control. I honestly don't think I can. I will literally die. You might as well stick me out in the snow storm to freeze to death. That would be a better death than to watch someone butcher my pate a choux recipe." My voice rose a few octaves as I expressed my disdain. Isla was clearly not moved by my speech. She gave me that mom-like look where her eyebrows knit together.

"But I hate that you have to spend every moment of the day here, Hollie." Her expression softened with pity. It almost felt like a hot knife to my gut. Did she really pity me? I had wanted to be a baker my entire life.I never got to go to culinary school like I wanted to but that didn't make me any less proud or happy to be here.

I hated that she wanted me to get help here, my controlling perfectionism would never allow anyone to even try to help. I couldn't even let Isla stamp the damn cup sleeves. How did she think I would be able to let someone even try to bake with me? Plus, I loved baking, I wouldn't have followed in our mom footsteps and taken over if it didn't bring me joy.

"UGHHHHHH. Maybe... Just maybe..." Yeah, there was no way I was doing that. But, if it makes her feel better, I can pretend for her sake. I could hire a high schooler to "help" even if that meant them doom scrolling their life away in the front while I busted my ass back here.

"Oh yay!" She clapped with joy, opening up her laptop again. The screen illuminating each ridge and valley of her face.

"Now that we got that out of the way we can go over the events for this year. We are doing the 12 days of Christmas, the candle light parade, Santa village night, snowmass sleds, the nativity festival ...." Her tone started to turn hysterical. I cut her off before she could plummet off the deep end.

"Isla, we do every event the town has to offer, plus the shop and every other order we get." I leaned across the table to grip her shoulders. I centered her gaze on me. This seemed to give her more motive to word vomit at me.

"Don't forget your cookie drive for the school, and then share a meal for the church."

"I know, alright, I know!" Not even the sweet peppermint latte was drowning out the annoyance of this conversation. Maybe Isla was right, maybe I do need help this year. *Yeah, like that was actually going to happen.*

"Alright, I will seriously think about it. I might go to the high school and check out their culinary classes. See about prospects." Her shoulders eased a smidge with whatever tension she let go in that moment. Her icy blue eyes glimmered with a glimpse of happiness.

"Thank you, Holls. Really, I appreciate it." She beamed at me. Well, as much as Isla could beam. Snow pitted against the window. The flecks melting away at its warmth. Even seeing some of her stress melt away with just the idea of me having helped twinged guilt in my gut. I just hated the idea of it all. A stranger in my kitchen, *our mom's kitchen*, baking our recipes, it just felt wrong. All of the recipes that stocked the shelves in this shop were either my mothers or mine. Countless hours have been spent curating each item. My mind reeled at the countless times I spent batch after batch, trying to perfect her recipes. Trying to make them just like hers, trying to preserve this last piece of her through them.

A shudder of cold ran through my body, even my thickest santa sweatshirt couldn't help from the invading chill from the frosted glass. The winter storm had crescendoed from a flurry to an outright cloak of snow. Outside, on the lantern light street, snowflakes rained from the sky like tiny stars. Through the darkness, the glow of the street lights illuminated a figure taking down the mercantile store sign. An older sign that had faded with age, its wood worn and cracked from the years of rain and snow.

"Surely that isn't Mr. Frost out in this weather making repairs." My breath is hot against the frozen window. My eyes squinted to make out who was dumb enough to get on a ladder in the middle of the night, in a snowstorm. The dark figure struggled to unhinge the oversized sign. Isla's coughing broke me out of my trance.

"Oh Hollie, I forgot to tell you at the town hall meeting." her words were meak.

The pit that was forming in my stomach knew something bad was about to happen. Isla never spoke to me that softly. Our eyes met for a moment, before she looked back down at her laptop.

"The Frosts are retiring from the store." She mumbled, as she pretended to be enthralled in work. My heart knew it was because she didn't want to disappoint. She still saw me as the blonde headed little girl that followed her around the town.

My heart sank a little at her words. Their weight unsettling my stomach. The old couple that ran the mercantile store had become some of our dearest friends, almost like second parents to us. Our mom worked very closely with them growing up. Often taking time to read to the children at their store. Our mom and Renee were determined to keep the Christmas magic alive within our town. It was going to be different with a new tenant across the street.

"You didn't think to tell me that earlier!" The mix of anger and sadness that boiled in my belly was coming out to lash at Isla. Hopefully she knew I was more mad at Renee and her husband than I was mad at her.

"I didn't want to make you upset, and I told them that I should be the one to tell you." Her tone went back to the normal stone that laid there. Impenetrable to the core.

"I will have to take some treats over with their weekly order on Sunday. They've worked hard, they deserve to enjoy their golden years." I paused thinking about not seeing their smiling faces every day. "I'm just going to miss seeing them all the time." I huffed as I plopped down across from Isla.

I honestly wouldn't know how to function without seeing Renee and Arnold daily.

"Me too, I really am sorry Hollie." She paused, her eyes softening with a kindness she only saved for me.

"Alright let's get into your mind this year, what are you going to make?" I started to drown Isla out as I watched the snow tinker down on the winter street.

Chapter Two

*P*ink satin bows laced around the stark white boxes on the countertop into neatly tied bows. The clear windows on the top showed stacks of sweet sugar plum danishes dusted with confectioners sugar. It was one of my most popular creations at the store. I had spent so much time perfecting the sticky sweet plum filling. Many hours of trial and error that ended with too many plums sacrificed and concrete mixing bowls. I tossed in an extra danish and a few extra new cookies I had created to the Frost's order. Arnold would eat them all before Renee was able to have any if I didn't. After fixing four extra hot sugar cookie lattes I settled them into the carrier. I always made the Frosts extra coffee with their order. Mr. Frost says he doesn't like all the "froo froo" coffee, then ends up drinking all of Renee's drinks.

The bakery didn't open until 12 on Sunday mornings, so I always made time to drop off orders and treats to some of my favorite customers. The Frosts only lived a short walk away from the historic downtown. Their house was in one of my favorite neighborhoods in Thistle Grove. In Yuletide Glenn all the houses here were planned around streets named after various yuletide themes. The Victorian architecture of the homes has been preserved through the years, with each owner adding a new flare. The colorful houses looked straight out of a book.

This was also the go to place to see the most over the top decorated houses for the holiday season. When we were little Rohen and Isla used to drag me through these streets to gawk at the lights. Snow crunched under my feet as I turned past the pink house on Partridge Lane. This had always been our favorite house to visit. The large baby pink house always looked like a glittering gingerbread village. However, it was completely bare now. A large for sale sign staked in its yard. I shook away the memories starting to bubble in my mind and made my way to the blue house at the end of the street.

The Frost's historic house was already garnished with rows of green garland filled with shiny baubles that resembled the color of snow and ice. Renee has always decorated the place so beautifully and had such a knack for details. The closer I got the more I noticed the icy blue nutcrackers and ribbons were sprinkled in. Mini Christmas trees lined the large white steps to their front porch. They too were spotted with the sparkling baubles. The stark white door had an emerald wreath of fresh balsam and holly. A single large white snowflake hung at the top of it. The fresh florals smelled heavenly. The silver Snowflake knocker on the door was cold against my fingers. *Thump, thump,*

thump, I clacked the door knocker against the door. The frame creaked open, Mr.Frost's white hair peeking through.

"Hollie!" his deep voice boomed as he barreled through the door.

His large arms wrapped me in a warm embrace, I finagled my arms to where I didn't drench us both in coffee. His pink cheeks were already rosy from the cold. The thick beard that coated his face was neatly combed, the icy blue sweater he had on complimented his snow colored hair. He always reminded me of Santa Claus growing up. I guess that is why he always dressed up for story time with the children at their store. Now in his older age, he seemed even more in his likeness. *I am sure I'm going to miss it.*

"Well don't be a stranger! Come in, come in!" He ushered us inside.

The Frost's home was just as beautiful inside as it was on the exterior. A large white wooden staircase spiraled to the second story of the home. It's carved railing doused in a twinkling garland of blue and silver. Renee's touches were sprinkled all throughout the entirety of it. A massive antique chandelier gleamed in the entryway. Competing for attention against the grand staircase. Each ring of it dripped with falling crystals, each one mimicking melting ice. Light refracted off the hundreds of crystals, casting the room in snowflakes of light, in true Frost fashion.

"Renee, Holly is here!" Arnold's voice boomed through the home.

His voice never knew a lower volume. As we trekked past the grand staircase and glittering lights I took in the glory that was their home. I basked in the glory of the custom wallpaper that blanched the walls, admiring each iridescent detail. My eyes roamed over the mix of artwork and photos on the walls as we made our way into the kitchen. My heels clicked loudly against the hardwood floors with the absence of the Christmas music that normally filled their house.

Renee was standing over the stove stirring something rapidly. Her sweater is the same icy blue as her husbands. Her long peppered gray hair braided down her back in one large plait. A brightly colored apron tied around her waist. It was clearly coated from battling whatever she was trying to cook. Bowls of something . . . were on the counter. The kitchen looked like a battlefield, and Renee was losing. My eyes met Arnolds, the same concerned look plastered on his face. Renee NEVER cooked. It was one of the reasons I brought them an assortment of breads and baked goods throughout the week. He shrugged at me and plopped down at the table with his latte and paper pretending to read to give us some space. Renee finally faced me, her face painted with a fake smile.

"Hollie, you might just be my saving grace." Her voice wavered with nerves.

It was not a common thing for Renee to be frazzled and it sent a wave of anxiety to my gut. Trying to ease her tension I jingled the two large boxes in front of me with a smile. Thanking the skies I had packed an extra treat box for her, hopefully it would remedy whatever mess was happening here.

"I actually brought with me the entire store, at least every item I'm selling this holiday season."

Arnold shot me a pitiful glance as I set the boxes down on the counter before going to inspect the war crime Renee was committing.

"Plus the sugar plum danishes I promised you." I added in his direction.He smiled at my acknowledgement of him.

"Oh, I knew she loved us." Arnold muttered into his paper with a smile.

"Hollie, everything has been a whirlwind this week, we had some unexpected news and then Rohen came back." She said as she whirled to face me.

Her eyes glimmered with the threat of tears. My heart panged at them, knowing it must be really bad for her to be crying. I had only seen her cry a few times, most of them involving Rohen not showing up for her. *Fucking dick.*

"Isla mentioned the store, but I didn't know Rohen was in town." I tried to keep my words steady at the mention of his name.

My heart fractured a tad for her at that moment because I knew part of her pain. Her only son, Rohen, did not want to be a part of their family business, instead he wanted to be an author. He moved to New York for school and never came back, not even for a visit. At least not until now. Renee wanted him to follow his heart but it hurt her to have him gone. Hell it hurt most of us to have him gone.

She looked at me with her eyes full of emotions. I could see the mix of grief and regret in them.

"Sweetie, I wanted to tell you, but I promise it was a last minute decision. Some health troubles are slowing me down. We're getting older and I just can't keep up anymore." Her voice was meak as they left her lips.

The tears magnified in her eyes at that moment. The only thing I knew to do was to pull her into an embrace. She wrapped her arms around me squeezing me back. The smell of dark vanilla and cherry perfume emanated off her. I savored her closeness. She was the closest thing to a mother I had left. I kept my arms around her until I could feel her heart slow from the hard pitter patter in her chest.

"I am sure going to miss you across the street but you and Arnold are welcome over anytime. Plus I can give you the senior discount now that Arnold's retiring. Someone is going to have to pay for his latte addiction." I couldn't hide the laughter in my voice. That seemed to bring a smile to her face.

"I am not addicted to any type of latte." He huffed from the table. Latte foam coating his mustache.

"I have time this morning, I would love to help with whatever you're doing. If you want some help?" I held up the plaid apron I had dug out of my bag. It matched my christmas plaid ensemble I had adorned myself in for the day.

"Oh heaven please. I haven't cracked an egg in almost 5 years and I am not sure how I was even able to turn them into cement." Renee smiled at me, the sadness in her expression fading.

"I would love to." I smiled back at her.

Christmas music played as she started picking up the clutter from the counters. I got work pulling down the ingredients I needed from her pantry and fridge. I already knew what I wanted to make and got to work breading some chicken. Time whirled past while I was cooking, it always did. Being able to show my love through my food was my greatest gift. The final timer beeped on the oven and I pulled out the finishing touches. Ever so carefully I plated the hot honey chicken onto some mini pimento cheese biscuits that were slathered in pepper jelly and goat cheese. Arnold had tucked a napkin into his shirt, prepared to demolish whatever I had made. He looked like he was about to eat a lobster dinner. They always made my heart chuckle, they were such beautiful people. It's hard to think that they were Rohen Frost's parents.

"Any reason you decided to make breakfast yourself Renee?" I have made most of their breakfasts for years.

"Rohen is here, staying with us." Her eyes couldn't meet mine as she said the words. I could feel my heart drop to my stomach. I hadn't seen Rohen since he left town without saying a single goodbye to me. Years of friendship, gone in a moment.

"That's so exciting, I bet you are so happy to finally see him." I tried to keep my tone cheer-y.

Hiding any flicker of emotion I was feeling. It had been years, I had buried that cross with Rohen long ago. I could tell she was already anxious enough. I grabbed an extra plate from their cupboard and made an extra plate for him. Trying to resist the urge to not draw a giant dick on his plate.

"Renee, if he gives you any trouble this time I will gladly shove some fruit cake down his throat." I imagined the thought of him, gagging on the fruit cake I knew he hated. Her giggle was stopped by the deepest voice.

"I don't take kindly to shoving things down my throat but thanks for the offer Holls." Rohen said from the doorway.

His voice had matured since I saw him. It had deepened, it sounded like smooth velvet now. The nausea building in my stomach threatened to come up at the sound of it. He winked at me as he ducked to get into the kitchen. My heart stopped beating for a second at the sight of him. Rohen was so muscular to be so tall. He was not at all the small high schooler I had seen before. His 6 foot 4 body had filled out in his absence. His chestnut brown hair was tucked neatly into place. The collar of his cream turtle neck was in stark contrast with his golden skin. His lush green eyes stared at me behind furrowed dark brows. His hands hung on the door frame behind him, slightly exposing a sliver of his stomach. He was the most handsome man I had ever seen, and I wanted to punch him right in his stupid face.

"Mom you didn't have to hire a chef for me, that's a little over the top." The tone of his voice nipped at me.

"Rohen!" Renee squealed in a condescending tone. "Hollie is here as our friend, we did not hire her." She glared at her son.

He simply shrugged and walked over towards where I was staking pastries on a tray. Of course he would try to belittle me. Why not when he has pretended I do not exist for the last ten years.

"Do you have any real food? " He exaggerated each

word. "I am not much of a sweet person." He said as he poked at the danish that his father loved. Propping himself up on the countertop beside me, he crossed his large arms across his chest. Watching my every move with his ever so sharp eyes.

"I bet you aren't." I muttered, chuckling at my own joke.

"What was that?" He asked quizzically.

"Oh nothing, Renee I am sorry to cook and run but I have to get back to the shop, I have to keep up with Mr.Frosts danish consumption." I offered her a warm smile.

"You have the bakery?" he questioned, "I thought Mrs. Winter ran that place."

"Rohen!" Renee tried to hush his tone.

It wasn't his fault. He wasn't in town to even know she was gone. Even after I knew his parents told him. I tried not to let the pain blooming in my chest peek through.

"She died while you were in New York." I kept my tone short, trying not to let the tears leave my eyes at the mention of her.

His green eyes scanned my face, trying to decipher the awkwardness that lingered between us.

"Hollie, I–" His mother cut him off before he could say anything else.

"Really dear, thank you so much for helping." She gave me a deep hug and a kiss on the cheek, and I headed out the door. That's a lie. I practically ran out the door.

"Thank you Hollie." Rohen shouted out the door after me. I couldn't help the anger that bubbled in my stomach. I had to figure out why the hell he was back in town.

Chapter Three

Four weeks until Christmas

*M*onday morning was always the busiest day of the week for us at the bakery. My apron in the dirty clothes basket was evident of the battle scene that lingered in the kitchen downstairs. It's pink and white stripes stained with an array of vivid frosting colors. Similar frostings and sugary substances smeared the countertops downstairs. The sheer volume of food I churned out this morning was a Monday morning miracle indeed. I absolutely hated Mondays. It was obviously the worst day of the week. Not because it was a hellish day for tourists. But because I despised having to frost cupcakes on Mondays. It was my least favorite baking activity.

The first week of December usually consisted of non stop Holiday activities, and this year wasn't any different. The town square had many Santa meetings, snow ball fights, wreath making, and lastly, the town's annual candlelight parade was on Friday. The mental pictures of what I was making reeled through my mind as I finished up my makeup. Today I went for the classic Christmas pink look. It was giving Clara from the Nutcracker vibes. My baby pink sweater had glittering gemstone and pearl snowflakes on it. I paired it with my favorite light wash denim that had similar gems and pearls dotted on the surface of the fabric. The snowflake earrings my mom gave me dangled from my ears, they were the perfect amount of diamonds and silver. I passed some rosy pink blush over my cheeks one more time before adding some pearls to my icy blonde hair for the finishing touch. Life was too short to be basic and I made sure I was anything but.

The walk to the shop was always quick. Especially since I lived in the apartment above it. The shop was still dark as the sun had not risen yet. Frost garnished the windows creating a veil of ice crystals on the glass. I normally started around four am on Mondays to get ahead of the day. Isla normally joined me around 8ish, leaving the mornings to myself. The sweet smell of espresso and peppermint always helped wake me up in the mornings. I did not care how many calories were in this drink, it was pure Christmas in a cup and it warmed my soul. Grabbing my planner I hopped up on the register counter ready to see the damage I had to do for the rest of the day.

December 3rd-

This weeks display

300 gingerbread men

200 gumdrop nest

200 Stained glass cookies

100 of each holiday cupcake...

The list droned on and on, plus Friday was the town's candle light parade to welcome the Christmas season. Maybe Isla was right, I might need some help. A sharp yelp in the darkness drew my attention away from the monstrosity of my day. Normally I was the only one awake this early, the other shops tend to open around ten or so. No one was crazy enough to be up at four in the morning when we had to stay open until well after sunset for the tourists. So it was odd for anyone to be wandering the street at this hour. Another sharp yelp shouted out in the darkness. I could feel my heart quicken in my chest. The street lights were too dim behind the frosted glass to see what or who was outside in this weather. Against my better judgment I let my curiosity get the best of me. *You would so get murdered first in a horror movie.* Tugging on my pink winter coat, I had to see what all the commotion was.

To my surprise, through the darkness and snow, I could make out a figure standing on a ladder across the street. I trudged through the snow and I was able to see that someone was struggling on a ladder. Dark denim trailed up the pair of long legs. A black puffer jacket matched the black beanie that topped his head. Rohen Frost. *Of course it was him dressed like the grim reaper.*

"Are you okay out here, I heard you yelping and going on, you're going to wake the whole street up." I chirped at him.

"Good morning to you Molly." His voice chattered, a sign he had been in the cold for a while.

He really was insufferable. We have been in every grade together from k-12. It's not like Thistle Grove was a large town. Yet the man before me was still pretending he can't remember my name.

"It's Hollie. Seems like you to forget everyone here." My arms crossed my chest as the annoyance I had for this man grew with each breath he took.

"I just wanted to see if you needed any help, I wouldn't have come out here if I would have known it was you." He muttered something under his breath I couldn't understand.

He did not reply, or even bother to look at me. His hands held in place a giant new sign that said "Frost Mercantile" in plain big black and white letters. Of course he would replace the red wooden Christmas sign that had decorated Frost's for over 20 years with this modern one. Even with my coat on, the cold had started creeping into my bones and I was not about to catch frostbite over Rohen. He doesn't seem like the type to take any help anyway. I turned on my heels to head back to the comfort of my shop.

"Wait." He called out with a pained tone. "I could use some help" He paused, "Please". I was shocked he even knew the word.

"Alright, what do you need? I don't have long or my hands are going to turn to ice." I snipped back at him. Keeping my replies as curt as his.

"Figuring you look like a giant ass gumdrop I find that hard to believe." He snapped at me.

"Excuse me! I thought you asked for help. It's not

nice to be rude to a person offering help, has no one ever taught you to be polite." I could feel the dismay rolling off him in sheets.

"Sorry." He huffed back at me climbing up another ring on the ladder.

"Can you climb up here and hold the bottom of the sign while I nail it into place?" His arms extended to the large sign he held in place above his head. It was absolutely massive, the thing had to be about four inches thick of solid wood. The weight of it could easily knock him off that ladder.

"Sounds easy enough."

Against my better judgment I stepped up onto the ladder climbing to the step right below Rohen. My hands reached up to hold the bottom of the wooden sign into place but I was wobbly. I was having to stand flush against his legs to be able to reach the sign. Wrapping one arm around his leg to steady myself I was able to secure the sign in place. I could feel how hard his legs were through the denim of his pants.

"Whoa! I asked you to help me not grope me." his dark voice rumbled.

"Unless you want the only baker in Thistle Grove to fall off and die, I am going to hold onto you." I yelled at him.

Being this close to him I could smell his cologne, a warm mix of salt and leather. It smelt heavenly. How could someone actually smell this good? I could feel the vibration of each hammer strike, bringing me out of my delusional haze.

"That should be good." He called with one final strike.

I retreated down the ladder, Rohen following after. We stared up at the plain industrial-esk sign. The look of accomplishment plastered on his face resulted in a smug smile. He was quite handsome when he was not being a total asshole.

"Of course you would want a plain white and black sign." I tucked my hands into my pockets, trying to get some relief from the cold.

"Not everyone wants to look like Christmas threw up on them, you know. This is classic." His eyes roamed over me as he said it. Making me feel the slightest bit of self consciousness bubble up with his stare. Another shudder of ice ran through me, I couldn't tell if it was because Rohen was such a grinch or just because it was freezing out here. This had to be one of the coldest winters yet to hit Thistle Grove. I could see the warmth radiating from the tinsel lit windows of the bakery. Pink peppermints and gingerbread men were painted with a slew of snow flurries on the glass. It looked like a picture straight from a hallmark movie, which I also loved. My heart sighed at the sight of it.

"Some people like the over-the- top Christmas spirit. It looks like you could use some." I poked his chest. " You're out here dressed like the grim reaper. Just waiting to kill some more Christmas joy."

He smirked at me as he whirled on his heels into the street. I watched his tall figure trek through the snow. Straight. towards. my. bakery. From the pit forming in my stomach I could already tell this was going to end badly.

"What are you doing?" The panic rose in my voice as I yelled after him.

I hurried up to him. His long legs had him a few paces in front of me.

"Well I thought you would want to invite me in for a cup of coffee to apologize for calling me... What was that again? The grim reaper of holiday joy." His voice had a mocking edge to it.

He had to be joking. My cheeks were roasting not only from his sheer lack of tact but the fact that he flashed me a stupidly handsome smirk as he did it. My mind wandered to the days of us as children, me following Rohen just like this through the white winter

snow.

Chapter Four

1 must be dead or having a horrible nightmare. Rohen Frost is sitting in my delightfully pink bubble of happiness staring at me while I make coffee at Five in the morning. Maybe this is what hell is like. It has to be. I let some of the steamed milk run onto my hand to see if I was alive. *Fuck that hurt.* The pain feathering across my skin told me that I was. Yet here he was, his long legs coated in dark denim with black boots were propped up on my table. He really did have the manners of a neanderthal. The black puffer jacket he had on had been hung up, revealing yet another layer of black. This sweater however was much tighter than the one he had on when I first saw him. This one was almost painted on, showing every curve of muscle beneath it. Then to top off his omen of death look, he had a black beanie, with his short brown waves spilling slightly beneath it. I couldn't stand to look at him. Rohen was looking around with his usual look of distaste. Surely judging the amount of "Christmas vomit" I had in the bakery.

My stomach growled in ever present silence. I was used to eating at 3-4 in the morning, being off my routine had every bone in my body fighting back at the deviation in routine.

"Do you want anything to eat?" My voice broke the silence. Even my enemies deserve the hospitality my mama raised me with. *Damn her and her pristine manners.*

"No, sweets are not really my thing." he said as he pointed to the case of sickeningly sweet pastries.

I chuckled at my own inside joke. Of course he doesn't like anything sweet. He told me the first time I saw him again with his parents. How times have changed. I could feel the familiar heat rising in my chest. I loved the essence of any challenge. What could I make him? I remembered the chocolate shipment I had gotten last week. I had the perfect thing to go with a dark roast espresso.

"Here you are, a midnight late. I tried to recreate something that matches your whole-" I gestured to his all black get up. "-deal."

He raised his eyebrows at me, his emerald eyes roaming my face. A hint of a smile tugged at his lips. Lifting the Old fashion Santa mug to his rosy lips, he hummed while sipping his drink. His eyes lit up in a sudden spark. I couldn't help but watch him as he recognized the unique flavor palette of the drink I had designed for him.

"It has the Cascade specialty dark in it with a hint of smoked sea salt. Your mom knows it's your favorite and asked me to make something with it. Not that you deserve it or anything."

Those emerald eyes locked onto mine. I tried not to squirm under his gaze.

"My parents seem to love you, but you are quite the little brat now." His lips smirked as they left his mug. His words left a bitter taste in my mouth.

"Coming from the man who hasn't seen his parents in almost 10 years and doesn't bother to call his mother, I could say a few choice words about you too." I had hoped my words were received with as much bitterness as I had intended.

I had not so easily gotten over the fact that Rohen left without saying goodbye to me. It showed our friendship was just the matter of who was there in the moment. However, him leaving without saying goodbye to Renee is a whole different story. I will never forget the look on her face when I showed up on their porch in the torrential rain. Showing her the text her son had sent me. She had almost fallen to her knees crying.

"You need to mind your own business." He growled at me. His voice darkened in warning.

I could feel the tension seethe out of him as he clenched his jaw. He deserved the awkward confrontation.

"I am rather fond of your parents, so excuse me if I have an opinion about the way their only son treats them." I said as I crossed my arms over my chest. Watching the muscles in his sharp jaw tick as he clearly ground his teeth.

"Back off Winter, I am not going to have this conversation with *you*."

Making sure to throw in a condescending jab with it. That is the moment I knew Rohen Frost was officially on my shit list. *Damnit.* I was not in the mood to have a debbie downer on my radar this Christmas season. I watched him raise the Santa mug to his lips again. He didn't deserve to use my santa mug.

"No." I curtly told him, snatching the mug from his hand taking the drink back to the counter.

His mouth hung open from literal shock. I suppose Rohen was not used to anyone being this direct with his asshol-y-ness. He was never told no as a child either which probably contributed to this attitude problem he has generated as an adult. The wooden chair screeched across the floor, the sound made my ears ache. The hair on the back of my neck tingled as I could feel him behind me. My pulse skyrocketed. *You are so stupid, calm down. It's freaking Rohen Frost. You mildly hate him.* I turned to face him, my back pressed against the wooden counter. Rohen's arms were on either side of me, his large body looming over me. He lingered inches away, his chest almost flush with mine.

Moments passed and neither of us moved. His emerald eyes burned bright as they stared down at me. The tension in the room was palpable. Strung taught like a live wire waiting to set off. The green pools of his eyes were flecked with tiny flakes of gold. They roamed down my face to settle on my lips. My heart was about to beat out of my chest. The rapid pace thundering beneath it. Rohen leaned closer to me, the smell of him was intoxicating. *Get a fucking grip Hollie. You haven't gotten laid in a while but we are not attracted to Rohen freaking Frost.* Lightly his lips brushed my ear and I couldn't help the gasp that let my lips. .

"I don't take kindly to being told no." His voice stirred butterflies in my belly that had long been silent. His hand snagged the Santa mug from behind me and he made his way out the door.

"That's my cup!" I shouted after him. *What the actual fuck was happening.*

"Bye Gumdrop!" He waved back at me, not giving me a second glance as he walked into the dimly lit mercantile store. That's the moment I knew I hated Rohen Frost.

Chapter five

Four weeks until Christmas

*T*he dough slammed into the quartz counter with a loud *bang*. I imagined each time I flipped it I was hitting Rohen right in his stupid face. Who the hell did he think he was? Coming uninvited into my bakery, then whatever the heck that was happening, and to top it off he stole *my* Santa mug. I flipped the dough again, slamming my rolling pin into it. Hitting the dough again and again, letting all my frustration out. I know I probably looked crazy to the customers peering through the window to the kitchen. The deranged baker that finally lost her marbles.

"Hollie, we have a shop full of people, I can see that you are taking your anger out on the croissant dough. But can we do this another time." Her voice was hushed, not wanting the forming line outside to hear her.

Isla slowly rolled the rolling pin away from me. Unarming me just in case I snapped. Which would not be surprising considering how much I work and my lack of social life.

"Are you going to tell me what is wrong with you and why you are trying to murder the croissant dough?" She stared at me quizzically.

"It's just I let Rohen Frost get under my skin this morning. Stupid prick. I just need to bake it out and I will be okay." I slapped the dough hard onto the counter with each word.

Isla just stared at me, surely trying to figure out how to diffuse me. I normally never got angry, or frustrated. I was always a Hollie-Jolly bundle of yuletide cheer. The perfect walking Christmas marketing campaign. Anger was something I hadn't felt in a long time. I wasn't sure how to even process it.

"Then now would not be the best time to tell you that Renee called and asked if you could take

over the holiday reading at the store for the week." Isla laughed as she said it. Trying and failing to ease my tensions.

My hands stopped working the dough and I gripped the counter as if I was hanging on for dear life. Trying not to let the slew of emotions swirling inside me come to the surface. There was no way I was going to be spending any more time today with Rohen. It was absolutely not happening.

"Are you fucking with me right now Isla. You were the one telling me I do not have time for anything and blah, blah, blah, and here you are adding more to my schedule." Nonetheless putting me in the same room as Rohen Frost. *My newly sworn enemy.*

"I will run the shop for the hour it takes you to read to the kids." She swatted at me, as if swatting away my ideas of escape.

How I wish I could say no. I wanted so badly for him to have to figure it out himself. Keeping the much needed distance between us. I couldn't let the kids down though, my mom always showed up, glittering gown and all to read at Frosts. Her and Renee kept the magic alive for all the kids that came to the store. Immersing them in a dreamworld with their stories. *I couldn't let her down.*

"You and Renee are lucky I haven't gotten to wear my gumdrop dress this year or this dough would be your face instead of Rohens." I can't believe I was actually going through with this.

"Alright Rambo, hopefully you can get your anger under control before you have to be in a room full of children." She grabbed her laptop off the counter and headed back into her office. At this point that thing was another appendage. We might as well glue it to her hands.

I hate to admit that I do truly love the Holiday stories Renee puts on each week. Watching the children circle around her with cookies in front of the fireplace while she whisks them away to a land of pure imagination was beyond magical. Hopefully, I will be able to live up to the legends of Mrs.Frost and mostly, Mrs. Winter.

I turned on our Pentatonix Christmas playlist letting the melodies softly fill the bakery. Isla clicked the lock on the door, and the sounds of Jingling bells rang through the shop with each customer that entered. With the amount of people we had puring in this week was already off to a busy start.

*   *   *

"Alright Miss Winter, it is your time to shine. Go get ready for story time." An almost evil glimmer plagued her eyes. Showing she did indeed enjoy my suffering.

Was it really almost noon? I couldn't believe the morning had passed that quickly. Half the cases were almost empty and we had restocked twice. We had to have over 200 people in here this morning. The town square was hosting a wreath making event this morning with a few other craft booths and it was packed. Isla was right about the excess people this year, it was going to be a challenge to keep up. Every day in December the town had something going on. That was part of the big draw for tourists. A picturesque town teeming with Christmas cheer. Thistle Grove was a scene taken right out of a snow globe. The line outside had shrunk but still was a steady stream trickling in. My skin itched at the thought of leaving Isla alone here for over an hour.

"Are you sure you're going to be okay here?" She could run the shop for a few hours, I just hated losing control of it all.

"Hollie, I know how to use the register and how to be a substitute barista. Plus it will slow down right now while all the activities are happening in the square. The rush will be right when you get back. You're favorite." She smiled at me. I guess it would be fun to step away for a while, even if it was in Rohens presence.

I ran upstairs to grab my dress and the story book for today. The dress was my mothers, she loved reading at Renne's. It was always the story of the Sugar plum princess. A book I keep on a stand on my bookshelf. Our mom had written and hand painted each page. Creating a masterpiece that seemed straight out of a fairy tale. In the theme with the story my mom had adorned a baby pink gown with hundreds of sparkles resembling gumdrops. I slid the gown on, the neckline hitting just below my collarbones. Showing the small snow flurry tattoo I have there. I had always loved winter, and that seemed the perfect tattoo for myself. The tight tulle sleeves sparkled down my arms. I grabbed the gumdrop crown and pinned it in place. The pale purple and pink gumdrops sparkled against the silver of the crown. As much as I wanted to not like it like Isla, I couldn't resist. I loved the over the top sparkles and magic of things like this. Our mom brought so much joy by living in the moment, it made me feel like her by doing it myself.

"Isla, you owe me for this." I yelled as I walked down the stairs. Her eyes were wide as she looked at me in the billowing gown. She wiped her eyes as she ran to hug me.

"You look just like her Holls. She would be so proud of you." Her voice quaked.

I forced away the tears that threatened the corner of my eyes.

"Now, Please try not to kill Rohen today." Her words teased.

I was not going to let the thought of seeing him again today ruin my mood. I was about to bring some magic to the children in Thistle Grove whether he wanted it or not. With a few hoots and Hollers from the customers in the shop I headed over red faced to Frost's. The bell on the door chimed its normal christmas tune, I see Rohen hasn't had the chance to take it down yet.

"Welcome to Frost's." His deep voice came from behind the counter.

He was busy checking out some customers and didn't seem to notice me. There was still about 20 minutes before the story time started so I meandered around the store, trying to see what he had done overnight. A lot of the displays had changed. The red towers and shelves were now a pretty stained raw wood. Cheesy Christmas decor switched for a more modern, more tasteful Christmas selections. Handmade candles, lotions, and other items still dotted the shelves. Just with more of an apothecary look to them. I took one of the candles down, smelling it. A deep gingerbread scent assaulted my nose. I was glad to see the products were the same, even if they lacked the Christmas razzle dazzle.

"If you are having a mental breakdown I can call someone to help you." I jumped at how close his voice was to me.

"Holy hell!" I slightly screamed. "You scared me half to death." Do you always stalk your customers?" I poked him in the chest. My finger hit the hardness of the muscles beneath his shirt.

"Only when they are dressed as a gumdrop sparkle ball in the middle of the day." His large hands toyed at the crown on my head.

"First of all, I am the Sugar plum princess." I swatted his hand away with my gumdrop wand. *God, maybe I do need some help.* "Secondly, I am here for story time. Hence, the Sugar plum princess attire." I spun in a small circle for him.

For the first time he looked stunned. His eyes wide as he was looking at me like a deer in headlights.

"Oh, I forgot about that actually, Mom left me calendars but it's so much in one week. They told me the store practically runs itself." He ran his hand through his hair. Clearly struggling with the change.

I couldn't help but laugh at him. Whole heartedly snorting laughing. The vein on his neck started to bulge, evident of his irritation with me.

"Would you like to include me on what is so funny?" His arms crossed his chest, a look of displeasure painted on his face.

Of course he wouldn't know all the effort that went into this place. He was never here. It took a miracle just to get him to cover the shop when we were kids.

"The fact that you believe that is so funny. Your parents are here from around five am to midnight every day of the week. That's why I always bring them meals, your mom does this and helps with all the volunteer activities with the church and food bank too. Or at least she was doing this. "

"I didn't realize.." His voice trailed off and he honestly looked kind of sad at that moment. I almost let myself feel bad for him.

"How could you, you're never here." I regretted the words when they left my lips. It felt a little too harsh, even if he deserved it.

"Well, thank you, I guess, for the Story time." He ran his hands through his short waves. Pushing them further back.

"I am doing this for Renee, not you, to make that very clear." I wanted him to know that I still did not like him.

"Crystal." He said with gritted teeth and headed off to make rounds with the customers. Finally, it seemed that I was the one getting under Rohens skin this time.

"Mommy! Mommy! She's Here!!!" I heard the squeal of the little girl running through the door.

The blonde little girl could have only been four or five and was clinging hopelessly to my leg. Her dress was a fluffy pink tulle similar to mine. Sparkles crusted her honey blonde hair.

"Adeline, honey, she might not want you to touch her." The girl's mother looked stressed, the small baby in her arms only a few months old. The large diaper bag on her other shoulder throwing her off balance. She was trying to juggle the rather large diaper bag, a stroller, and the wiggling babe in her arm. I gave her a warm reassuring smile trying to ease her nerves.

"Adeline, that's such a beautiful name. Are you here to read with me today." I squatted down to her level, letting the little girl run her hands all over the gems of my dress. *God squatting like this is killing me, I really am getting out of shape.*

"Yes! I even brought my own wand, see!" The little girl held up a star gumdrop wand covered in ribbons and glitter. The same kind my mom used to make in the town's craft-a-thon each year.

"Adeline, do you want to help me set out the cookies for all of our friends today?" The little girl bubbled over with excitement. Jumping up and down next to me.

"There is a quiet room in the back where your mommy can take your little sister while she needs to eat." I smiled at her mom.

"I wanna be a helper!" Her wide eyes gleamed up at me. She laced her fingers within my own.

"Are you sure? You do not have to do that?" The woman looked at me, while Adeline stayed latched onto my side.

"Pleaseeee, mommy." Her eyes threatened tears at the hint of the word no.

"There are drinks and pastries in the back. Enjoy some quiet time, I would love to have her help me." I could see some relief instantly meet her shoulders.

I couldn't imagine being a mom. It was a lot of work to take care of myself, much less two other humans that needed me constantly. My heart was happy to be able to help her.

"You are too kind, thank you so much." Hey amber eyes softened as she spoke. Her littlest babe pulling at her fiery red hair.

She gave her daughter a quick hug and headed to the back of the store. I took the little girl's hand again and led her to the story time area. A large white antique velvet chair sat beside a roaring fireplace. The stone work reminded me of an old English cottage. The old stones varied in color and jutted out imperfectly as they cascading up the wall. A rather large vintage looking rug garnished the floor in front of the fireplace. The walls were covered in newspaper articles about Santa from around the world. Large white marquee lights read "Frosts" across the wall. Hundreds of glittering newspaper snowflakes hung down from the ceiling, it truly was magical.

Little Adeline helped me dish out plates of snowflake cookies I had made the morning before. They were sweet simple sugar cookies. One of my mothers favorites. I sat back in the large velvet chair as large groups of kids piled into the store. Little Adeline sat right beside me, tracing the gumdrops on the train of my dress with her tiny fingers. I was so nervous just to read to these kids. Their parents huddled around all smiling at me. I could feel another pair of eyes boring into me. I glanced up and my eyes met Rohens, he was staring at me, surely criticizing my every move. I couldn't let that distract me. I broke our gaze and readied myself in true Sugar Plum Princess fashion.

"Alright boys and girls, who is ready for a story about the Sugar Plum Princess?" I pulled the large leather bound book from behind me. Its cover was crusted in a sea of large gemstones.

The children squealed with excitement before me. Once the plates of cookies were passed out it was finally time to begin our tale.

"Once upon a time, in a kingdom from another land. A castle made of sticky sweet gumdrops rested on the diamond hillside....."

Once the story was over the children moaned and groaned not wanting to leave. Honestly, I didn't either. I wish I could stay the Sugar plum princess instead of Hollie Winter. But that wasn't the reality I lived in. Hopefully Isla hasn't burned the whole bakery down while I was gone. We said our goodbyes and I started to clean up the hurricane of cookie crumbs. Footsteps broke the silence in the room and I already knew who they belonged to. The smell of his leather and salt cologne giving away his identity.

"You truly are just an explosion of Christmas vomit, Miss Winter." Rohens' voice mocked me as he started to collect the plates and cookie crumbs off the floor.

"Coming from Mr. Joy killer himself, I think my christmas spirit level makes up for the lack of yours." I retorted back.

"Have you always done this at the store?" He asked as he continued to clean the floor.

"No," I paused, "You know my mom used to, she even made the dress, and the book." I shoved the memories down that were trying to escape. I didn't want to cry here. Not in front of Rohen.

"Well, you are quite good at it." His words were fragmented. Odd in their delivery, but a compliment nonetheless. *Did he actually just compliment me?*

"Careful Rohen, if I wasn't too sure I would think you were actually being nice to me."

"Not a compliment, just an observation." Of course it was. He huffed.

We continued to clean up in silence. The bustle of the shop seemed so far away in this room. I really hope he left this place alone. This was the one room that had never changed in Frosts.

"Umm, would you want to keep helping with the story time thing? I can't seem to muster up an all black Santa suit." his lips curved into a soft smile, something I was shocked to see from him.

Did he actually want me to keep doing this for him? Not that I didn't love it, I was just surprised he would want me here that much.

"I can only come twice a week, On Sundays and Thursdays." *Why are you volunteering, like you have time?* I'm sure the repercussions of this would eventually come back and bite me in the ass.

"It's alrig-. Wait did you actually say yes? For someone that shows their disdain for me I am surprised you actually agreed to help me." He was sitting on the edge of the fireplace, looking at me as if I was a strange animal.

"I might need help with my Sunday deliveries, but if you can help with that then we have a deal. Also, I am not doing it for you." I chimed, trying to make myself seem uninterested.

His eyes stalked my movements. His large frame was overtaking the fireplace. The black button down he had on was tight against his skin. The dark jeans he had on this morning were still neatly tailored to his tall frame.

What did I just sign myself up for? Isla was going to kill me. I could see her head exploding as I told her the over commitment I had made.

"Sounds like a deal." He outstretched his hand, I gathered my things quickly. I did not need any more physical contact with Rohen Frost today. I was almost out the door when Rohen shouted after me.

"I'll see you Friday night gumdrop!" I couldn't stop the butterflies that swelled in my stomach.

Chapter Six

"*O*h Isla!" I chimed as the door to the bakery shut behind me.

The bakery was bustling again, the line was wrapped around the store. Electricity started to run under my skin when I realized just how fucked we were. The cases were scarce, and it was surely not enough to feed the line of people behind us. *Fuck! I knew I shouldn't have left.* Isla and Renee were moving at lighting speed behind the counter. The old silver cash register *Chinging* off the hook with each guest.

"Thank heavens you're back!" Isla was visibly stressed,more than usual, the sweat pouring down her face, a key indicator that she was probably about to melt down. *Double Fuck.*

"Give me five minutes." I shouted as I ran up the stairs needing to put on my baking clothesShe nodded in reply. Grabbing clothes I pulled on my jeans and instead of a sweater, I pulled on a baby pink tank top. Even with this weather outside the bakery would get up to almost 80 once I turned on all the ovens. Plus I like seeing the snowflakes that dotted from my collar bone down to my wrist.

Hurriedly my feet flew down the stairs, pink snowflake apron in hand. I closed the shutters to the kitchen, blocking the view of me scrambling like a beheaded chicken. Once out of sight I ran, frantically pulling everything off the rising racks that were ready for the ovens. Thank heavens I put in four ovens a few years back or we would we would be super fucked. A symphony of movement began, chocolate croissants and puff pastries were in one oven while I rotated batches upon batches of cookies and cupcakes in the other ovens. After an hour I had fresh hot pastries ready for the rest of the line that still seemed to be growing outside Hollie's.

I pulled a few more trays ready for the oven and started working on frosting cupcakes that had cooled. Isla stepped into the kitchen, slowly. Surely wary of how I would react to her after springing the reading act on me this morning and not getting me when our shop was about to be wiped clean.

"Listen Hollie, before you start." I pointed a piping bag at her, ready to douse her in frosting. She took the hint and let me talk. Leaning back against the work counter behind her.

"Why do you think I would be upset Isla? Could it be that we almost sold out everything I had made for the next three days? Or could it be.. Ummm.. the fact that Rohen is going to be at the Candle light festival with me and you didn't seem to infirm me." I squeezed the piping bag so hard icing coated the cupcake and oozed onto the table. A sigh escaped my chest.

"You know we are always paired with Frost's, I didn't put you with Rohen on purpose Hollie." She frowned at me, the displeasure evident by my accusation. I know she didn't do it on

purpose. It just felt that the universe was trying to test me with the amount of Rohen Frosts I was having to take.

"This is the world's way of getting back at me for all the times I faked being sick so I wouldn't have to volunteer at the high school isn't it." She chuckled at me.

"Look, I know you are less than fond of Rohen, but he is here to stay. Or at least that's what Renee said. How do you think it affects her to see her like-daughter mortal enemies with her only son. You two used to be somewhat of friends" She crossed her arms giving me her best mom look.

"You know that's different now." *Crap.* I wasn't thinking about Renee or what she would think about it. Surely he has not told her I don't like him. Renee is like a second mother to me, I can't believe I didn't even think about that. She was already anxious about him being back, and here I am just creating more drama for her.

"No, I honestly didn't, now I feel terrible."

"She chalked it up to stress, Holls. It's okay. Is there anything I can do to help?" She gestured to my orchestra of chaos happening in the kitchen.

"Those trays on the left are ready to be put back into the cases." My piping bag pointed to the 12 stacked cart of trays.

"Holy shit Hollie, how did you just do all of that?" Her voice cracked.

"I had prepped way more than needed, just in case. Thank snow I did or else we would be closing right now!" I could hear the panic in my voice. "Are you two okay up there making drinks?" The thought of Isla trying to grind an espresso bean made me anxious. Coffee was not her foretay, they would end up getting a cup of chunky diesel fuel.

"Yes, thankfully we've only had hot cocoa and cider orders, or else we would have had the Sugar plum princess making coffees." Her lips cracked into laughter. The thought of me in a gown and crown making lattes cracked me up too.

"Hey, I was a great Sugar Plum Princess thank you very much. It was very magical." I twirled and bowed with my words to give her the full effect. I wasn't lying about that either. Seeing all those kids' faces light up while reading to them made me beyond happy.

"I hope you had fun, I heard about your agreement already, after you yelled at me for Jamming up your already tight schedule and *With* Rohen of all people."

"I didn't think I would have as much fun as I did. Honestly, I felt closer to mom doing it. That story is one of my favorite memories of her." Our mother would have loved to see me following in her footsteps. She wore that dress amongst other costumes anytime she could. Trying to create Christmas magic for everyone around her. *Plus Rohen left me alone.*

"I know Holls, Me too." Isla's face softened. Her forehead creased lessened and she actually smiled at me. My big sister was often only business, and a large ball of stress. Trying to make sure we had enough overhead to function properly, retirement accounts, insurance, all the work. She needed something to focus on once mom died and this was her way of taking care of us.

"So do you believe me now that you need an assistant?"

"I do, but how am I going to teach someone how to bake everything when we are going through three days worth of product in a single day. Maybe today was a weird freak accident. It's a monday and they had activities all day, there has to be a reason we were booming today."

Throughout the week I had just found out how wrong I was. Monday was no freak accident. It was just the start of the busiest season we have ever had. We were almost tripling our sales each day. It wasn't just us that had felt the wave of people, the other shop owners were having the same problem. They were running out of inventory faster than they could have it delivered. The week rushed by in a flash. I had gone into hyperdrive trying to keep us stocked for the week. I didn't even realize that it was finally Friday, the day of the Candle light festival.

Chapter Seven

*T*he morning frost was even more harsh than usual today. Now, I love the cold, but today the bakery was an iceshop when I got up this morning. The old buildings' windows couldn't hold back the frigid winter air that seeped in. I pulled a cropped sweater over my icy blue bralette before I headed down to start my morning production. Waking up at three in the morning was normal to start baking to prepare for the weekend. Most nights I honestly wondered how little I slept. With a flick of a switch the lights whirled on, bringing the twinkling wonderland to life as I started my first morning espresso. Even with the ovens on I was glad I had pulled on some fuzzy socks and house shoes. This is what my normal mornings looked like. Baking in my sleep deprived state in my pajamas to have enough stock to supply this mob-ish crowd we have this year.

A thousand candle shaped cookies stared back at me as I drafted out my plan for attack. These cookies were going to go fast tonight, they always do. The sweet cranberry orange cookies were topped in a special orange-vanilla royal icing decorated to look like a candle. With a glittering edible gold foil flame. I loved this cookie, year after year, I never changed it.

I was mid-sip when I heard the door bell jingle. My heart thudded hard in my chest. Isla wouldn't dare roll out of bed at this hour. I was almost sure I had left it locked when I opened up this morning. Grabbing the heaviest baking sheet I could find I stealthily creeped to the front of the shop. Trying to keep my movements as silent as possible. *Surely no one would want to rob a bakery. Are you dumb Hollie? Of course someone would wanna rob you. You live upstairs on top of thousands of dollars in baking equipment.* While my inner monologue battled itself, I mustered up the courage to round the corner from the kitchen. I let out a scream and I collided hard with another body.

Cold hands wrapped around my waist keeping me from falling into the floor. *If you're going to get murdered at least they're a polite murderer.* My eyes snapped up to meet a flustered Red faced Rohen Frost.

"Were you about to clobber me with a - Baking pan?" His eyes glanced at my choice of weapon.

"Yes, yes I was, because I thought you were a murderer! Who just breaks in at three in the morning! I'll tell you who, MURDERERS!" I poked him in his stupidly straight nose. He looked slightly irritated at my gesture.

"At least I know to leave the door locked, anyone could have come in here, and you're wearing..*that.*" His eyes roamed my body looking over my choice of attire. "Do you always bake in such skimpy attire, you might be attracting the wrong clientele"

The wrong clientele? Who the hell was he to tell me what I should or should not be wearing in MY house. I was so angry at him I had yet to realize I was still entangled in his arms. His cold hands were placed on my hips where my sweater did not cover the skin. Quickly, I shoved myself an arms length away from him. He almost looked normal without his usual all black modern facade. He was wearing gray jogger sweatpants that fit low on his hips. The blue columbia hoodie accented the muscles of his arms. *Ugh, Stop looking at him like that Hollie. We are not about to check out Rohen Frost.*

"Well, Rohen, What is it? I am in my pajamas because it is early as hell, not that I have to explain that to you. What do you want at three in the morning? I have an entire day to prepare for plus I need to prepare myself for the disaster of a night we are going to have."

His emerald eyes grazed up my body, making me aware of the sheer lack of clothing I had on. I crossed my arms over my chest, at least trying to cover up some more. He toyed with his hair, his dark brown waves framing his face messily.

"Actually, I saw you were up and I came to see if you would make me a cup of coffee and we could talk about tonight." The nerve of this man.

"Are you bailing on me?" The sinking pit in my stomach made me nauseous, was I actually upset thinking he wasn't going to come with me? "I understand, I figured it was not your vibe."

I tried to mask the disappointment in my voice. It was tradition for Winters and Frosts to go to the Candle light festival together. Helping lead the town in the winter festivities of the night. It was also one of my favorite town gatherings as they had the annual gingerbread competition. I loved seeing everyones recreations, plus tasting all the treats was a big win in my book.

"No. I am going, I just..." He paused. "My mom wanted me to talk to you about what I need to wear and all of that, she said to at least try since you have done so much for the shop." His hands anxiously wove through his hair.

This was him trying. Breaking into my store and telling me to make him a coffee at three in the morning.

"Are you actually going to wear something that is not your normal black, modern day reaper attire?" I raised an eyebrow at him.

Was Rohen actually going to do something...nice for me?

"I can at least put in an effort, I am not guaranteeing anything here." His tall frame leaned against the doorway. "I am sure you will be in a full Christmas tree costume or something of that nature." He winked at me. Now he was mocking me.

"Has anyone even explained to you what the festival is or anything in that nature?" My eyebrows raised at him.

"You forget that I grew up here too Hollie, I can handle shaking a bell in the parade. I am not an idiot." How could I forget it? Our childhood days we followed each other around like shadows. Stealing cookies from my mom and running through town getting into anything we could. It started to change when we went to high school. Rohen became more reclusive. Focusing on his writing, and his plan of leaving us all.

"It's not the same as when we were kids Rohen, you can't just run off after the parade."

"No-why? Should I be worried?" *Hell yes you should.* I am pretty sure that much holiday activity would be Rohens kryptonite.

"Ugh, I'll get us some coffee and go over the changes from the past few years. But you're going to have to sit or something back here. I have to get these cookies iced for tonight."

He followed me silently to the front of the store. He leaned against the door frame watching me as I made the two of us some fresh coffee. I made his new usual, or at least I decided it was his usual. Putting the salty dark chocolate into the cups for the espresso to pour over. I had been leaving one for him with Renee each morning, So I assumed he drank it. He nodded at me as I handed him the steaming mug.

All of my piping bags sat in a neat colorful row on the island. Each one full of sparkle dust. I grabbed the first one and started to outline all of my cookies. Rohen stayed silent, watching me intently.

"So, this festival you and I are paired up to sort of welcome in the new Christmas season like our parents used to?" He hopped onto my clean countertops, I made a mental note to sanitize it after he left.

"They are more elaborate than what you were used to. There are a ton more booths open now, and an ice skating rink, carolers, and there are going to be lots of contests and all of the shop owners judge them and score them. The highest scores of the night are ranked Yuletide Queen/King of the season." My hands held the piping bag tightly as I worked over the cookies.

"Sounds delightful." I could practically hear the sound of his eyes rolling at my explanation.

"There will be music, vendors, a pageant, dancers, Santa and his reindeer, the whole nine yards. It is a very joyful event so do not bring your Christmas killer attitude, okay?" Hopefully Rohen could put on a show just for the evening.

"Mhmmm." He muttered. His concentration on his drink instead of me. *Of course he was ignoring me.* I waved my hands to get his attention. Nothing. He was still intently staring at his cup.

"Hello, earth to Rohen."

"Why have you been leaving these with my mom each morning? I told you I didn't like sweet things." He was still entranced by his coffee.

"Did you hear me about tonight?" The irritation was starting to peek through my voice. He really doesn't take any of this seriously.

"Yeah , I heard, don't be a christmas killer blah, blah, blah. I don't really care. I want to know why you keep making these for me?" That is what he's focused on. The damn drink. This conversation was going nowhere.

"How about a thank you Hollie, for making me a latte as dark as my soul. That is so nice of you when I am a ginormous dick." I shouted at him. I should have poisoned his damn coffee, then I could just worry about myself this holiday season.

"It is, for your information, but I am having to fucking run an extra three to four miles to keep up with the fucking sugar in this." An extra three to four on top of whatever he was already doing? Holy shit, I could barely make it up the stairs after busting my ass down here all day much less go do some kind of freaking crossfit hell.

"For your information, you acted like you liked it when I made it for you the first time. So I've sent one with your mom ever since. I do not see anyone forcing you to drink it." I pointed a piping bag at his chest. "Maybe you should learn how to have some self control." He opened his mouth and actually laughed at me.

"Me? have self control? Coming from the human fucking gumdrop, thats rich."He curled over he was laughing so hard. It made my blood boil. I slammed the piping bag down and red frosting shot out all over my icy blue sweater.

"Fucks sake." I pulled the sweater off and immediately threw it in the sink, hoping the hot suds would salvage it. Knowing the kind of dye I use, this sweater was a goner.

"Hollie." Rohen cleared his throat as he said my name.

I was left standing there in my silk pajamas shorts that already had half my ass out, and now a lacy bralette that barely covered my breasts. Heat rushed to my face in embarrassment. I had just stripped in front of Rohen without thinking. But he wasn't looking at my breasts, his eyes scanned up my arm and onto my collar bone, tracking each snowflake and frost that dotted my arm. I watched him swallow hard as he met my eyes again.

"I'm sorry, normally I am by myself and I can just rinse stuff out when it happens." I babbled on. Rohen did not reply, he simply stared at me. His eyes are dark, and his body tense. I wondered what he looked like under that sweatshirt. *Snap out of it Hollie!* He stepped closer to me, leaving almost no space between our chests. I had to get out of here before I did something I would regret.

"I am going to run upstairs and grab a new shirt, it will just take a second." I forced the words out.

I practically ran up the stairs to my bedroom to put some distance between us. I can not believe I just did that. I haven't gotten laid in a while, but does that rule out my absolute dislike for Rohen? Hell no. He was a handsome man, but I still loathed his presence. I rummaged through my closet trying to find some kind of lounge wear that didn't have half my ass out.

"I figured your apartment would be more maximalist than this." His voice made me almost jump out of my skin. My head hit the shelf above me in surprise. *Fuck that hurt.* He really doesn't have any kind of inclinations about boundaries.

"The whole weirdo, breaking in thing, you're doing it again." I snapped at him as I rubbed my head.

Rohen plopped down on my bed propping himself up on his elbows to look at me. His long legs slightly hanging off the queen size mattress. I kept the sweatshirt I had pulled down clutched to my chest.

"What can I say, I let my curiosity get the best of me. I am honestly in shock that you do not have 50,000 Christmas trees up here. I was expecting Santa's village, some elves, maybe 8 tiny reindeer." He smirked at me.

Seeing him on my bed turned waves in my stomach. His hair messily laid over his emerald eyes. His t-shirt is riding up just below his gray sweatpants. Rohen may be an absolute dick but he was fine as hell. *Stop looking at him.*

"You are such a fucking dick do you know that?" The words flowed from my mouth, It felt good to finally say it to his face.

"Excuse me?" He adjusted himself to be sitting on the edge of my bed.

"YOU. ARE. A. DICK. Rohen Frost." My steps took me closer to him with each word letting the sweatshirt fall from my hands. "You come back into town with a holier than thou attitude because, for some reason, your joyful parents birthed a christmas hating psycho who thinks he is too good for Thistle Grove." A small smirk tugged at one side of his lips, his eyes locked on mine.

"Admit you like me." His words lit my skin on fire. His eyes burned into mine. The nerve of this man. Me? Actually like him. He practically torments me on purpose, and is the complete opposite of my entire being. How could I possibly begin to like him?

"C'mon gumdrop, I want to hear you say it." His words teased me, the tension between us was building to breaking point.

"I do not like you, Rohen Frost." He rose off the bed, his body towering over me. The man was an almost seven foot giant. Growing up I had imagined a few scenarios of Rohen in my bedroom, but none like this.

"Say it again, for me" He winked at me while his fingers brushed my chin. *Holy gods, what the fuck is wrong with me.*

"You are absolutely insufferab-"He cut me off with a soft kiss.

His lips brushing ever so gently against mine. I took a step back, breaking the kiss. My pulse was pounding beneath my skin. Everything was on fire. I am not sure what possessed me at that moment. I shoved him back onto the bed. Or at least he let me think I did. My legs straddled his waist, his hands roaming up my thighs. I leaned down to kiss his lips again, this time with more force than he had kissed me. It was pure lust. His lips opened for me and I explored his mouth with my tongue. The taste of dark chocolate was still on him from his drink earlier. My teeth nipped as his lower lip elicited a small moan from him. I was instantly drenched at the sound of it. I could feel him through his sweatpants beneath me.

"Rohen." His name slipped off my lips. He flipped us so fast that his full body weight was pinning me to the bed. I squirmed underneath him. His large fingers pinned my arms above my head. His lips kissed each snowflake up my arm devilishly slow. His hips pinned mine in place, leaving almost nothing but the fabric of his sweatpants between us. His lips left a trail of fire up my arm until he reached my ear.

"Admit you like me." He whispered into my ear, causing my hips to arch in response.

"No, gumdrop. I want to hear you say it." This man was about to have me undone by simply talking to me. His lips met mine again, barely tracing the outline of them.

"Fine, I fucking like you Rohen. I wish I hated you but I can't." My voice barely a whisper.

"I know you do," He whispered into my ear. Just like that he was off of me, adjusting himself and heading to the door.

"Rohen!" I called after him.

He paused in the doorway, his chest slightly heaving.

"Frost looks good on you Gumdrop." He winked at me. I tried to yell after him but it was too late. He was already headed down stairs and out the door.

Chapter Eight

The rest of the morning at the bakery was a whirlwind. My regulars dotted the faces of hundreds of people I did not recognize. It gave me little time to even try to think about the events that happened this morning. As the rush slowed down we were able to regain our bearings. The cases were stocked, the floors were clean, and the line had dwindled to a slow trickle of customers. The next in line was a strikingly beautiful woman. Her fire red hair complemented a set of hazel eyes and freckled skin. She reminded me of the summer sunshine. Lyla Farrow. One of the most popular girls in highschool and that seemed to continue into our adult lives. Her family owned a speakeasy style restaurant in the square, it was one of the classier places in town. More of a Rohen city man type of vibe. I had a few dates there and somehow Lyla always ends up dating whomever I seemed to bring there. Whenever I saw Lyla, drama normally followed in her path. *Great.*

"Hollie, it is so good to see you!" her red lips smiled at me, leaving her extraordinary white teeth gleaming back at me. As much as I wanted to dislike her, I couldn't keep away. She had that effect on people.

"Good morning Lyla, what can I do for you today?" Hopefully my fake smile would be enough to evade her from whatever she wanted from me.

"Well, I wanted to invite you to a small gathering at 1920 to help kick off this winter season with all of us younger business owners." She handed me a black card with gold calligraphy lettering. It had a 20's deco style theme to it.

"It sounds great Lyla, I will try to get away." I lied knowing that it was going to be impossible to leave for an entire afternoon. Lyla didn't have to know that though.

"It's going to be cocktail attire." She gave me a once over, "Absolutely no frosted

clothes aloud." She winked at me. Sometimes Lyla could be really great, she was fun and full of energy. It's just that she channeled that energy into her mean girl endeavors.

"You're friends with the Frosts right?" I sensed a favor tagging along with this question.

"Yes, Why?" She piqued my interest.

My gut already had a feeling where she was going with this. A new prospect she had not yet conquered was in town. It didn't matter that Rohen was breathtakingly handsome, Lyla would want him anyway.

"I wanted to invite Rohen, He's back in town and looks absolutely yummy don't you think?" She giggled at me. "He was always sought after in high school and it just seemed to have followed him as he aged. I am going to see if he wants to be my date, but if for some reason he says no, help me get him to come. I will owe you the grandest favor, Hollie." She battered her perfectly placed lashes at me.

Suddenly I felt sick, of course she was going to try to snare Rohen. Another notch for her next man eater conquest. I mustered up my fakest smile and shook my head. My morning breakfast threatened to come up as I watched her walk over to Frosts' a box of pastries in hand. Good thing Rohen didn't like sweets.

I finally let out a breath, having to grip the counter for balance. *Get your shit together Hollie.*

"Hollie, are you okay?" Isla was staring at me, her icy blue eyes scanning me like a hawk.

"I'm fine Isla." I tried to keep myself neutral because I didn't want to admit to her or even myself that I was actually starting to like Rohen Frost.

"It looks like you are about to upchuck all over the place."

"I'm fine." I was clearly not fine. I had admitted that I liked Rohen and let him freaking shove his tongue down my throat this morning.

"What did Lyla ask you to have you in such a tizzy." She came closer, hopping up onto the counter.

"She basically invited me to a party where she is going to try to bring Rohen as her date."

"Sounds like Lyla has found her next conquest. The real question is, why do you look so upset about it. I thought we didn't like Rohen."

"We don't. I don't." I tried to reassure myself. It clearly was not working. I tried to not let the thought of Lyla and Rohen consume the rest of my day. It wasn't hard when a returned box of pastries landed on my counter attached with a note.

I already told you, sweets are not my thing, gumdrop.

*   *   *

"Holy smoke show!" Isla yelled at me from the bathroom door. Her body draped in a long pink robe, with a matching towel on her head. "You look smoking hot, Hollie."

I glanced over myself in the long wooden mirror that adorned my closet. The cream ribbed knit dress clung to my body in all the right places. The hem hit just above the ankles with a classy slit running to the tip of my knee. The neckline was a soft v, hitting my chest at just the right spot. My icy blonde hair was curled in large voluminous waves. A crown of garland and red ribbon encircled my head, small white candles dotted its rim. I matched my lipstick to the same shade of red as the ribbon, the deep scarlet made my lips look extra plump. I went for simple diamond-like drop earrings, and topped the outfit off with a pair of tall booties. I knew I would need a coat the darker it got but with the heaters the town put out and all the walking I should be fine. *Or I would catch frostbite.* I slipped on a pair of thermal lined panty hose just to be safe.

I fiddled on my phone doom scrolling until Isla finally emerged from the bathroom. She chose a cardinal red ensemble for the night. The matching red sweater she wore was dotted in pearls. A large pearl headband pushed back her curls. The cream wide leg denim she paired with it was so cute.

"Isla, you look absolutely merry!" She flipped me the finger

"Thanks for letting me raid your closet, I was sure the queen of Christmas would have something I could wear." she gave herself a final once over in the mirror.

"It's actually the Sugar Plum Princess, but I forgive you this time." I chuckled sitting on the edge of my bed playing with the beading that lined the comforter.

"You know Hollie, I saw Anthony in the shop today. He was asking about you?"

"Anthony - firefighter Anthony?" The blonde firefighter was relentless. I had shooed him away attempt after attempt and he would not take the word no as an answer.

"Yes, he wanted to drop in, see if you had any fires that needed to be extinguished." She titled the curling wand around like a ding dong. Her words bursted with laughter. I chucked my peppermint pillow at her and we started to head out for the night.

"Like I have any time to date anybody, much less Anthony. Who has, let's see, been on a date with every woman in the entire town-including you." I told her

"Maybe you will meet a tourist and fall in love like a hallmark movie. The small town baker meets the big city blah,blah,blah" She pretended to swoon.

"Okay now that you're delusional, so plans for tonight, one of us has to bring home some of Edna's spiced eggnog or I will go on strike."

"Noted, where is your co-judge?"

"I told Rohen I would meet him at the tree, If he actually shows."

"Good luck with that, It's going to be like the grinch when he is made the holiday cheer-mister." I pictured Rohen getting shoved faces full of food and grandma kisses.

"I never asked you about why you wanted to be extra cheery tonight, are *you* meeting someone tonight?" She instantly blushed as red as her sweater.

"June asked me to date tonight, I didn't want to make a big deal about it." Her voice meekly faded away. June was Isla's high school crush. A beautiful blonde, with bright blue eyes. They became a doctor and work at the clinic in town with Dr.Morales.

"She is super cute and her volunteer work makes her even hotter."

"God, I know. We volunteered at the elementary school together for the vaccine clinic and we just hit it off." Isla seemed giddy for the first time in years. Grabbing my coat from the door, I clicked the lock into place behind us.

"I hope you let loose and actually have some fun." I winked at her resulting in the big sister glare I knew all too well. She gave me a parting hug and walked down the street towards the clinic. I took a deep breath to steady myself. I was not going to let Rohen Frost kill my Christmas cheer.

Chapter Nine

Thistle Grove was glimmering with hundreds of Christmas lights. The street lights were adorned with large wreaths with a single white candle in the center. The symbol of the candlelight parade and the oncoming winter. The store fronts were decked out in garlands and gadgets. Enough to make the town look straight out of a story book. In the center of the square a large tree towered over the town. Its branches decorated with a multitude of glimmering colorful ornaments. Its light illuminating the square. Speckled around the massive tree were rows of wooden booths full of holiday vendors. Each one curated to perfection for the night. Almost all of the shopkeepers set up a booth as well as some out of towners. Christmas melodies fluttered through the air mingling with the bustle and chatter of the night. The winter chill had slightly dissipated, making it bearable to be in the sprinkling snow.

This night was always so exciting for the town, the official start to the Christmas season. The bloodline that fueled our ever growing community. Everyone was out here, the crowd melded into a sea of people. I scanned around the tree looking for Rohen in his full black garb standing out like a sore thumb. His black toboggan was nowhere to be found. A small pang of disappointment threatened to push at my chest, but I brushed it aside. I was not going to let it ruin my night.

"Well, well, look at you Hollie Winter, as beautiful as ever." The familiar voice cooed at me.

I turned to see Will -Mayor Sanders- dressed in his finest winter garb flashing an oh so charming smile at me. His blonde hair was neatly cut and placed. His cream sweater complimented his tan skin. He had a smile that lit up a room, his presence often seemed to draw attention. Will had always been the super star athlete center of attention type guy. It was no surprise he ended up being the Mayor. He actually was really invested into the community and wanted to keep this town alive and well. He took my hands and brushed a small kiss to it. His lips were a warm whisper against my skin. Leaving behind a small trace of his cologne.

"William, It is always good to see you." His blue eyes were so striking against his tan skin I couldn't look away. I could feel the blush rise to my cheeks.

"I miss seeing you in the mornings, you know."

"I think you were abusing the delivery method just to get me to bring sweets to your office so I would talk to you." my hand brushed his arm as I stepped closer. *Was I flirting with him?*

"That's not such a bad thing now is it? A smart, beautiful woman, who happens to be the best baker in the entire town showing up in my office once or maybe three times a day. You can't blame me." His smile has always been so warm. His oh so perfectly straight teeth flashed at me as he chuckled. It was a warm and deep laugh.

"I'm glad I got to see you tonight before you were sucked into your Mayoral duties William, really." I leaned in to give him a light departing squeeze knowing he was going to be swept away.

"I'm going to try to find you tonight once things settle down, maybe we can schedule my next office delivery?" He winked at me, sending blush down my entire body. I could feel myself grinning as I swiveled to head off towards the start of the parade. A large body bumping me to a halt.

"So sorry, I ..." My words trailed off as my eyes roamed over the large biceps I had been holding onto. The familiar leather, salt, and vanilla scent tickled my senses. Rohen had actually shown up, and not only that, he was in a bright red sweater. I gave him a quick once over. Dark denim hugged his legs, and a sleek pair of brown chelsea boots were on his feet. But he had actually put on a vibrant red garment. Even with the loose style of it, hsi arm muscles stretched the fabric of it and I could not stop staring.

"You came...I .. wasn't sure if you had bailed or not." I tried to not let the disappointment seep into my voice.

"I have to do this for my parents, I just couldn't find anything to wear." Not doing this for me, noted. This morning had just been a quick lapse in his judgment. And mine.

"You look nice in your festive sweater." I softly smiled at him.

"It's not festive, it is just plain red. Not related." He stepped back, breaking our touch. Glad to see Rohen was still as cold as ever.

"Who was that , that I saw you drooling over you." irritation laced his voice.

"It was Willi-Mayor Sanders, why?" He shrugged, tucking his hands in his pockets.

"The same Mayor Sanders that just cut the funding for the shelter here?" His expression started to change, he looked pissed. *Where had that come from?*

"Nevermind, Let's just get this over with, I have to finish the new displays at the store."

"I hate to burst your bubble, but this is an all night affair. At least until midnight. We went over this this morning." I tisked at him in annoyment.

" I was a little distracted this morning, sorry if I didn't retain all of the details." he said as his eyes were watching my lips.

So he obviously didn't forget that I had straddled him in my bed this morning. *Great.* We trailed through the crowd to the start of the parade. Rows and rows of out of towners lined the streets. Bundled up waiting for the magic to start. The tiny mountain town had a small snow slurry brushing its streets. Coating us all in flecks of the frozen crystals. It always made my heart skip a beat to see the excitement on their faces.

" Not the simple Santa parade throwing candy like it used to be, huh?" He looked over the sea of people.

"No, Will has been a big part of the growth of our town. Along with social media and Etsy, it has been able to help so many places stay open even with the transition of the new stores.

"I didn't realize you were on a first name basis with the mayor." He still would not meet my eyes.

"Will is a big reason all of these people come here, Rohen." I retorted at him.

"Those people are just sucked into the monetary aspect of christmas." He really was a peach.

"Rohen, all of these people are here because they think our town has something special. That we have built some place magical they can escape their lives and come step into for a moment." I was honestly surprised that as a writer he couldn't see the draw behind it.

"I wish I could live in your sugar coated reality gumdrop." He looked at me like I was a hopeless child. Rage boiled in my stomach.

We spent the next two hours circling the town square. The parade was headed by the Thistle High band, rows and rows of horns and drums snaked in a delicate cadence. Majorettes followed in suit, their red and white uniforms glittering under all the lights. Eight rather large reindeer pulled a shiny red sleigh. Mr. and Mrs.Claus inside, Rohens parents, waving to the passing crowd. Jingle bells played as they strode threw. The businesses followed suit with white candles burning in the night. A long line of decked out parade cars trailing behind us. As we neared the end of the line, my face hurt from smiling so much. The ache in my heels shouted at me to have worn different shoes. Rohen's face stayed its normal stoic, mysterious look. Only giving out a few small smiles here and there.

The sun had finally set, a red haze still lingering over the small mountain town. Everything was aglow with the hundreds of Christmas lights that decorated just about every surface. Wooden booths had been constructed all throughout the square, the huts hosting a variety of items. My stomach growled as visions of hot cider and soft buttery pretzels penetrated my thoughts.

"Have you eaten today?" Rohen asked me, while vigorously typing on his phone.

"No, I have been a little distracted today." He looked at me quizzically. Before he had time to respond, Lyla approached us. Her red hair braided into a crown on her head. Showing off the beauty of her face. She barely paid me any mind, her focus on Rohen. Honing in on her target.

"Well Rohen, You look handsome as always. It's so nice to see you participating in this season's festivities. I hope to see you around town more often." Lyla was laying it on thick for him. Batting her eyelashes at him. Reaching out to slightly embrace his arms.

"It's nice to see you again, Lyra." Her smile threatened to turn sour. I could feel the displeasure rolling off her. Lyla was not used to not being showered by male attention.

"It's Lyla. I guess I will have to stop by more often to help you remember it." she purred while fully grabbing his arm. "We have some catching up to do, since you've been gone. I want to hear all about your publishing business in New York. I am having a get together soon at 1920 I would love for you to accompany me." She added an even more seductive tone to her voice. A predator on the hunt for its prey.

My stomach growled again, even louder this time. Rohens head snapped towards me. Lyla's eyes were sending daggers at me. Pissed that I had interrupted the opportunity.

"It was good to see you, but I am afraid I have to take Hollie here to get something to eat before her stomach eats itself." He stepped away from her grip, snaking a firm arm around my waist.

"I'm sure we will run into each other again. See you later Ly-rah" He called to her as he drug me away, her face as red as her hair with anger. She looked like she was about to explode.

"I have never seen her so angry at being turned down before." I told him as he ushered us towards the food section of the vendors. He seemed to ignore me as usual.

"You really haven't eaten anything all day. Are you trying to pass out?" His voice raised.

"That is not your concern." I huffed at him, prying his hand off my hip.

"The fuck it isnt." He growled at me. "Tell me, gumdrop, what do you want to eat?" He said as he gripped my chin.

I was nervous someone would see us. Not that I was embarrassed to be seen with him. Just, that I probably look like a mess. The way he asked me had me falling apart all over again. How could his damn voice do that to me? I swallowed hard.

"I usually always get the soft pretzels and cider, it's my second favorite." I mumbled

"The favorite?" He asked.

"It's not here anymore." I twiddled my thumbs thinking of my mom standing behind her booth soft butter cookies in hand.

"Fine." He said curtly retreating back to his phone.

I can't believe he is actually mad at me. After the events of today, I should be pissed at him. Rohen grabbed my hand, leading me to the hot pretzel booth. Edna, the sweet older lady that ran the booth each year, lit up when she saw my face. The delicate lines of her skin truly showed her age, but I always thought she was beautiful. Long white tendrils curled in kinky twists that surrounded her face. Her dark skin complimented her light amber eyes. Those eyes followed my hand to see who it was attached to. Instantly, her face dropped a little as she saw Rohen Frost at the other end of my finger tips. Edna had been in this town long enough to know the hot spots for gossip and she always seemed to indulge.

"Rohen Frost, I heard you're back in town. Hopefully, to stay this time?" She refused to make eye contact as she bagged up the most buttery, overly salted pretzel bites she had. Picking out the pieces she knows I love. Rohen fidgeted anxiously as she slowly worked through the pretzels.

"That's the plan so far Mrs. Edna." he replied, her eyes not leaving mine.

"For you Hollie." She handed me the bag with a smile. I took the bag fumbling to pull out my wallet.

"You are not paying me Hollie Winter. That's final." she said with such vibrato.

"Edna, you have to let me pay, please." She shooed away my outstretched hand.

"No dear, I do not. Enjoy, I'll make sure to save the extra buttery pieces for you when you come back around." She winked at me.

"I would eat the entire booth if you'd let me." I chuckled at her.

Rohen has disappeared at some point in our conversation. Probably ditching me, I didn't even care at this point. These delicious pretzel bites are all that I need. I meandered through the booths, spotting a tall red blob making its way towards me, two ciders in hand.

"The fact that they charge $8 a piece for these is highway robbery." His long arm outstretched one of the steaming ciders. I could smell the caramel and cinnamon wafting from the cup.

"You're helping support a small business, Gale that has that booth each year, is the librarian for the town and the school. She helps bring in all kinds of books and activities to the schools.That Cider booth helps pay for that." His face softened.

"I didn't know that." He ran a hand through his tousled brown hair. His go to stress induced movement.

"You've missed a lot since you've been gone." I sipped from the warm paper cup. Mmmm. I had missed this.

"I can't enjoy my drink with you staring at me like a creep. Did you poison it, is that why you're watching me?" a small laugh left his lips. He glanced at the rolex on his wrist.

"It's almost time for the gingerbread competition." He said.
I dusted off the salt crumbs on my hands.

"You're going to need that drink, some of them can be very...dry." I imagined him choking on some of the dry crumbly houses.

"Perfect," he grumbled.

Chapter Ten

*P*erfectly crafted houses lined the tables ready to face judgment day. Their theme this year was to accomplish creating Mrs. Clause's bakeshop. I strolled between the tables, looking at every detail. They were absolutely beautiful. Table seven, had an unlikely fondness for my shop. Well at least the gingerbread version. A cute pastel pink themed shop sat with a very generous coating of edible glitter over the whole thing. A small gingerbread lady was outfront, a pink and white snowflake apron just like mine. The windows were lit aglow from inside the structure. They had even recreated the garland I made for the store. I wanted to take it home with me.

"Egotistical much, Gumdrop." Rohens voice was barely a whisper behind me. Trying to keep our conversation just between the two of us.

"You're just mad someone did not recreate you in cookie form." I poked at him.

"Mhmmm. I am sure that could be arranged." I couldn't help the blush that crept up my cheeks. I guess he decided to let some of the joy defrost his attitude a little bit tonight.

We walked through the tables once again, the mayor announcing that it was finally time to taste them. Pieces of the houses were broken off onto tiny napkins from each booth, I was itching to try them. A good gingerbread cookie is timeless. Table by table, Rohen looked almost green as we tried the cookie pieces. Each one slathered in a menagerie of royal icing and toppings. I found that scraping the icing off to taste just the cookie is the best go round with these competitions. That way you didn't feel like you were going to upchuck by the fourth house. Unlike myself,

Rohen Frost did not take that approach. He was eating the icing, glitter and all. *Ew.*

"Are you okay? You look...rather.. Well, awful." I asked him in between our next to last house.

"I feel fine, this thing is almost over then we're done." His words were shaky and breathless. "Do you have any water?" he asked, his voice slightly shaky.

Hell he did not look good. I nodded and passed him my bottle, he chugged it in seconds. We walked a few steps to the last house. The bakery, my bakery, was the last house of the night. Rohens steps staggered as he walked to the table gripping my arm for steadiness. .

"What the hell is wrong with you, are you drunk?" I whispered into his ear as I intertwined our arms steadying him. He pulled his phone out, struggling to pull up whatever app he was looking at.

"I need to get to the store, now." He said as he looked at his phone.

He swallowed hard as he looked at me, his skin was clammy even in the cold night air. I wanted to protest. I wanted to show him I could be an ass hole too. But looking at him I could tell something was really wrong with him.

"Carrie, I will be back soon, please turn our clipboards in. The mayor is going to have to find someone else to announce the winner." The ginger haired girl grabbed the clipboards from me staring at the now hunched over giant I was half carrying.

"Yes Miss Hollie!". She replied, giving me an okay sign. She was one of the cutest girl scouts I had ever seen. She often came with her mom to the shop on the weekends.

I wanted to be angry at him , of course he would ruin the night. My gut feeling told me that something was off with him. It dulled the anger in my chest slightly. He didn't protest as I stayed attached to his side, keeping him balanced. We walked down the snowy street together, the town lights fading in the distance.

His hand trembled as he pulled his keys from his pocket, fumbling trying to unlock the door. I helped him steady his hand and turned the lock with him. He really wasn't looking too hot right now. His golden skin is now a pasty white. His vibrant emerald eyes hooded in a haze. There was no snarky banter leaving his lips. Only shallow breaths.

"The couch." He panted out. He was starting to really scare me.

"Okay, Rohen, you are starting to freak me out. What is wrong with you?"

"Leather bag behind the counter." His head relaxed back over the edge of the couch exposing his neck. I hurriedly grabbed the leather bag and rushed over to Rohen. He lifted his shirt to a small pod on his stomach. Fumbled trying to pick at the tape with his shaky hands. I gently placed my hands over his.

"Let me help." My voice was barely but a whisper. I peeled the tape off and Rohen was able to pull the pod off his stomach. He opened his eyes and inspected the small white device.

"Fuck!" clearly pissed at whatever he had found. He grabbed his phone and pulled up an app. A bright red number popped up on the screen. 475. I handed him the bag he requested and he pulled out something that looked like an epipen. Clicking a dial at the top he stabbed the needle into his stomach.

"Rohen, do you need me to call someone? I can leave if you want me to.."

"Stay." His voice was gentle. "Please." his voice was barely a whisper.

It felt odd to watch him at this moment, clearly panicking.

"I didn't know you were diabetic." The parts started to click into place.

"I told you I do not like sweet things." A small smile tugged at his lips.

"That is not really telling someone you have a medical condition." I thought back to the events of the night so far. Rohen had a giant caramel cider and at least 11 gingerbread cookies smothered in icing and gumdrops. I lightly smacked his arm.

"Hey, no hitting until I feel a little normal okay. I would like to be 100% when you decide to punish me." He tried to tease but his voice was still a whisper. He still clearly felt like trash.

"I can't stand you." I told him.

"Mhmmm, that's why you drug me back here."

"I dragged you back here because you looked like you were about to fall out. I thought the cookie competition was actually going to kill you. Too much joy for your icy heart to handle."

"The needle in my pump bent, so I was not getting the insulin I needed to eat all of that trash. I still would have been high, but not that high." He said. "I was using my app to try to give myself a correction dose but it didnt do anything because my pump was fucked."

" Is that why you're grumpy all the time because your blood sugar is high?" He glared at me.

"I am not grumpy." he mumbled as he unfolded the kit on his lap. His hands slightly less shaky.

"Oh no! I forgot you are just a perfect ray of sunshine." I pretended to gasp in shock.

"Watch yourself, gumdrop." he stood up and flung his sweater to the floor. My eyes wandered over his body. Rohen Frost was more than hot. His sculpted muscles were god-like. I'm sure from how many hours he spent running and torturing himself. He plopped back down on the couch. Even sitting you could see every curve of his abs. *Gods.*

"Are you trying to take advantage of me during a medical crisis?" his thick eyebrow raised at me. A smirk played across his lips. He knew he was damn playing me.

"Rohen!" My voice came out four octaves higher than normal.

"Calm down, I am putting my next site on the back of my arm. His hands worked gently cleansing his arm and unwrapping his supplies. "My shirt will be back on in no time."

Taking a vial of what I assume was insulin and measuring it out putting it into a small device. A small click and a new pod was on the back of his arm.

"Good as new." he winked at me. "You can go back Hollie, I know tonight was important to you." A hint of sincerity coated his tone. *Maybe Rohens heart wasn't frozen after all.*

"I want to make sure you're okay. Are you going to stay the rest of the night by yourself?" *Not that I should care.*

"I rather like my toes so no more sugar for me tonight. I'm fine. I just need to drink some water, and wait for my meds to kick in. Maybe walk around a little. Some light Marathon training." He winked at me.

Is he serious? Even if it wasn't Rohen, I wouldn't be able to sleep if I didn't know he was okay.

"Well, if you don't want to go back out to the festival, at least come over to my place, so I can watch you for a few hours, to make myself feel better." I waited for him to deny me, to tell me I'm crazy. I was shocked when he went to grab a backpack behind the counter. In that moment I knew I was absolutely fucked.

Chapter Eleven

*T*he best thing about living above a bakery is the incredible smell. My apartment permeated a perpetual warm vanilla scent. I knew after high school I wanted to live here and help take on the bakery full time. I basically gutted the whole thing once mom moved her office. It was a quaint two bedroom place. The second bedroom was on the smaller side so I used it as my office. Or my excuse of an office. It was mainly a room for all of my books. Whenever I had free time, I loved to read.

The mauve pink tones echoed through my apartment, it was so girly I loved it. I decided not to theme my living space and just collect what I actually liked. Turns out I like the color pink and copious amounts of books. Rohen looked out of place as he wandered around my apartment. His tall frame was dressed in his traditional black garb. The black really crashed with the pink vibe I was going for.

I let him make himself at home while I went and showered. The devil on my shoulder wanted to drag him in with me. But I couldn't read Rohen. I was still trying to decipher whether this was a game to him or if there actually was chemistry between us. I let the hot water run over my body, washing away the stress in my shoulders. Once I was thoroughly scalded I slipped on a pair of my most conservative pajamas. A pair of icy blue silk pants with a matching camisole. I would burn up in this later, but Rohen would be gone by then.

The apartment was awfully quiet when I stepped out of the bathroom. Rohen probably realized his disdain for me and snuck out. *Typical.* The door to my office was cracked open, a dull light appearing from it. The door creaked open and Rohen did not bother to acknowledge my presence. He was panning through my shelves. The floor to ceiling bookcases were a beautiful raw wood. Making the books that adorned their shelves stand out.

"I didn't take you for a reader? How do you even have time to?" his fingers gliding over the titles on the shelves. It felt intimate, the books I picked were a part of my personality. The places I wish I could go, the person I wish I could be. It felt like he was going through my diary.

"You never asked." I mumbled.

My love for reading grew when my only friend had left me utterly alone in this town.

"You have some beautiful first editions. I am not much of a fan of the sprayed edges, but some of these are very nice." His back was still too much as he rummaged through my shelves. I knew he went to school for English and worked at a publishing house, but Renee didn't give much more than that. After my own sleuthing I realized he had started his own publishing house. He had written multiple books. I had them all on my shelves.

"See anything you like?" I wondered what his style was. He seemed like a non-fiction kind of person. *A true psycho.*

"Surprisingly, I actually do. I like high fantasy- so game of thrones, the witcher."

"So like the fantasy smut books." a giggle left my lips.

"Those are not smut books, these are smut books." He waved his hand over my shelves.

"Are you smut shaming me, Rohen Frost." He turned around to reply but he stopped mid sentence. His eyes were trying to melt me with their death lazers.

"I am just pointing out that a large portion of your books are fairy smut." His eyes roamed my arm, following the intricate lines of black ink.

"You are a smut shamer, how disappointing." I tsked at him. He moved on to the next shelf, stopping in the middle. A black book was fitted on a small golden book stand. The golden letters pooled into the word Frost on the cover. It was the only time I had heard from Rohen after he left. It wasn't much. He mailed me a copy of his book, signing it to his old friend.

"You kept my first book." His tone was quiet.

"Of course I kept your book." What did he think I would do with it? Burn it? I should have, I was so pissed with him.

"I didn't think you got it, you never said anything." his fingers rummaged through the flags I had placed in his book. Marking each page I found interesting or quotes that I loved. Rohen was a talented writer. He just wasn't good at real life relationships.

"Are you serious? You left without a word!" The anger was rising in my chest. He sat the book down on its pedestal turning to me. His eyes darkened.

"Like a thief in the night she left me breathless, our story never ending, regardless of our departure. My heart searched for her."His voice was deep with an emotion I couldn't quite place.

I always wanted those words to be about me. They sounded even more dramatic coming from Rohens lips. To think he didn't forget about me here. Tears threatened the corners of my eyes. I felt his cool hand lift my chin up, his lips barely an inch from mine.

"It has always been about you, Hollie." His words left me breathless. The air punched from my gut. *This had to be a fucking dream.*

"Tell me you like me, Rohen." I felt confident in my stance. I was done playing games with him. I wanted to hear him say it.

"I fucking like you Hollie." His lips crashed into mine. His arm ensnared my waist pulling me into him. I was probably going to regret this in the morning. But right now, I needed Rohen. My arms wandered up to his neck, his hand gripped my thighs and hoisted me around his waist. Fuck he was strong.

He pressed my back up against the door, showering me in kisses.

"I need you to tell me you want this before anything else happens here Hollie."

"Rohen, I want this. I want you." He kissed me even deeper than before, his tongue swirling around mine. I arched my hips into him, wanting more friction. His hands palmed my ass, leaving me wanting more. Without setting me down he knelt down on his knees, not breaking our kiss.

"Stand up for me." he asked, his emerald eyes looking up at me from behind his brown messy hair. I watched as he pulled his shirt over head, leaving nothing to block my view from his sculpted muscles. His hands tugged at my waist band. Asking for permission. I slipped my satin pants off, tossing them aside.

Rohens hands massaged my thighs working their way up closer to my ass. The tension was killing me. He nudged my knees open with his lips. Placing soft kisses trailing up my thighs.

"Rohen." I moaned beneath him, I could feel myself dripping down my thighs.

"I have waited so long to taste you, Gumdrop. I am simply going to devour you until you scream my name." His tongue flicked my clit, sending a shockwave through my entire body. His arms cradled my ass and sat my legs over his shoulders.

"Rohen, I'm too heavy."

"Shut up, nothing about you is heavy." He silenced me with another sweep over my clit. My hands yanked his tousled hair. My hips arched into his face with another moan.

"Fuck you taste so fucking good." His tongue moved in circles around me, leaving me whimpering above him. Two fingers slipped inside me, I bucked at the friction. I could feel the coil in my belly tightening as Rohens fingers pumped in and out of me.

"That's a good girl, you are so fucking perfect."
I couldn't stop the gush between my thighs, Rohens tongue dipping in to taste me. His tongue moved in slow circles around my clit, nipping and sucking in just the right places.

"Come for me, gumdrop." His emerald eyes were locked onto mine, watching me ride his fingers. I felt myself explode around him, in an earth shattering climax. I rode his fingers until the waves of pleasure subsided. Soft kisses dotted my thighs, as Rohen unentangled us.

He got up from the ground, placing a gentle kiss on my forehead. I grabbed his head leading him to the living room. The room was softly lit with the white warm glow of the christmas tree.

"These need to go." I tugged at the hemline of his jeans, and he quickly dropped them, kicking them aside. He truly was glorious. He was so huge I had no idea how it was going to fit inside me. I gently shoved him back on the couch. He grabbed my legs pulling me down with him. I was flatly laid on my belly across his lap. His palm rubbing my ass.

"Tell me Gumdrop, have you been a good girl?" I looked back at Rohen, as he loudly spanked me. My ass stung where he had hit my skin. I could feel his cock twitch beneath my belly.

"Fuck." I moaned, biting my finger ready for the next impact. His hand smacked my ass again, slightly jolting me forward. My ass was going to be bruised tomorrow.

"Your ass is so perfect, tell me what you want." His hand trailed to the wetness between my legs. My desire clearly showing.

"Fuck, baby you are so wet for me." His fingers slipped out of me to deliver another hard smack to my ass.

"Chapter 35 of your first book." I blurted out. I could hear him chuckle behind me.

"As you wish gumdrop." He moved us in front of the Christmas tree. I kneeled in front of him, his giant cock was daunting in front of me. He pulled the hair away from my face. I slowly took his cock into my mouth, swirling my tongue around the pre cum that had pooled there.

"That's it baby, you take this cock so nicely." He moaned the more I took him into my throat. His hands grabbed my hair into a fist, pumping himself in and out of my mouth. With what wouldn't fit in my mouth I used my hands to work him. I gagged on the length of him, my eyes watering as he fucked my mouth. *How the fuck was this supposed to fit inside me.*

He moaned, his hips moving more frantically. I gripped his cock harder, twisting my hands to make him come faster. His movements slowed down, letting me swirl my tongue around his cock. Bobbing my head deeper and deeper. I could feel him twitching in my mouth, I knew he was so close to cumming. With one hand I grabbed his balls, while I took him as deep in my throat as I could.

"Fuck!" He shuddered over me, his cum spilling out of my lips as I tried to swallow every drop.

"I hope you're not tired Frost, I have more plans for you tonight."

"Oh do you now?" He stroked my hair away from my face.

"What would that be?"

"Let me show you." I pulled him to the floor. The glow of the christmas tree illuminated every curve of his muscles. I traced his abs with my fingers, trailing down each one until my hands reached his cock again.

"Do you have a condom?" He froze

"No, I didn't expect this to happen tonight." He gritted out.

I knew I was going to fucking regret this. I straddled him bare, looking at his face for permission. His hands gripped my hips, his eyes burning into me the entire time. He slowly tugged on me pulling me down on him. I could already feel his girth stretching me with just the tip of him. His eyes were locked on me. I didn't break our gaze as I slowly lowered myself halfway onto his cock. He stretched me so much it burned. I winced a little at the contact,

"Hollie, are you okay?" His voice was soft but horse with desire.

"Yes, I'm okay, I am just trying to fit you inside me." He moaned as I slid the rest of the way down his cock. Leaving no space between us. I put my hands on his hard stomach, I needed something to give me leverage. I lifted my hips and grinded into the blissful friction his cock was bringing me. His hips rose to meet my movements. I rocked against his cock, he was hitting the perfect spot inside me every time.

"Baby you take my cock so fucking good. You took it all baby, you are such a good fucking girl." His words made me fucking soaked, I rode him even harder.

"That's it, gumdrop, ride my cock." His hands roamed up to my breast, his thumbs circling my nipples. The friction was driving me mad. He quickly moved to a sitting position. Just deepening the depth of his cock inside me. I moaned at the contact. He used one arm to prop himself up, the other gathered my hair behind my head and pulled. Leaving my neck exposed.

"Are you going to come for me, again."

"Yes." I whimpered as he slammed his cock into me again. With a cry I shattered on top of him, I could feel his thrusts become less controlled, more erratic. He moaned as he emptied inside me, causing me to rock and moan at the sensation of him. We laid on the floor in front of the christmas tree, falling asleep in a tangled mess.

Chapter Twelve

My blaring phone alarm assaulted my ears, starling me awake. *3:00 AM* the bright numbers glared on the screen. *Ugh.* I rolled over to enjoy my regular 15 minutes of doom scrolling when I bumped into a rather warm body. I practically jumped out of the bed. My eyes scanned over the rather massive body that was draped along my bed. Seeing Rohen passed out in my all pink bed made me realize that last night was not a sugar induced fever dream. It was real, evident by the soreness between my legs. *What the fuck did you do Hollie.* Trying to muster up the strength to get up and shower I quietly rolled out of bed to not wake him up.

I plopped a salted honey shower steamer into the bottom of my tub, turning the hot water on, letting its scent fill the bathroom up. I stepped into the water, letting it run over my body. How did this even happen? I knew I had feelings for Rohen, hell he made me tell him I liked him. But, it never felt reciprocal until last night. The events of the evening reeled through my head until the click of the bathroom door snapped me out of my haze. Rohens soft footsteps filling the silence.

"Can I join you?" His voice was laced heavily with evidence of his tiredness.

"You can, but I am going to warn you I like the water extremely hot." Rohen stepped into the shower and it was just another reminder of how god-like his body was. Water bounced off his toned skin, running down his pristine abs.

"Good morning." he smiled brightly at me, It felt like I had whiplash from his emotions. I never knew which Rohen I was going to get. Hopefully after last night, we have some steadiness.

"Good morning, Rohen." He pulled me in for a gentle kiss. Letting the water fall over us.

"You're up very early today." he grabbed the shampoo and started lathering my hair. It felt divine.

"I am the only one who bakes for this bakery so I have to be up to be able to get everything done."

"That doesn't seem sustainable, do you really do that?"

"Yes I really do, I have a time management system planned out and it works to get everything in and out of the ovens on time. How did you think we had so many supplies here."

"I honestly thought it was the fairy princess gumdrop magic." His comment made me laugh.

"You are actually cutting into my time management system right now." He took the shower head and massaged the shampoo out of my hair.

"Oh, am I?" He sprayed me in the face with the water.

"Rohen!" I smacked at his arm.

"What is it, gumdrop? I leaned back into his carved chest, letting his body support my weight. His free hand roamed over my body creating suds with the vanilla scented soap he found. The other hand kept us in the stream of warm water. His fingers began to wander, creating bubbles on my chest. His hands trailed down to my breast. Circling my nipples with fingers causing me to arch into him.

"Tell me Gumdrop, do you ever play in the shower." His question sent a shiver down my body. Honestly that was the whole reason I had bought that shower head. I was alone and not about to hook up with Anthony the firefighter just to get off. I leaned my head back and nodded. He clicked the shower head to the jet setting. Its powerful stream made me squirm.

"Open your legs for me." I propped one leg on the edge of the tub, giving Rohen full access to me. He slowly brought the shower head between my legs. The pressure was amazing, it sent tingles down my spine. I rocked back into him, missing the friction that I had craved from him last night.

He was so close to slipping in, I rocked my hips feeling the tip of his cock nudge my entrance. He slowly rocked his hips, allowing the head of his cock to barely push into me. I couldn't help the moan that left my lips. As sore as I was, I wanted him again. I needed to feel him stretch me like he did last night. The shower head was blasting my clit, sending wave after wave of pleasure through me.

"I am so close, Rohen." I slid further down his cock, feeling him stretch my entrance. Rohens hand pulled my hips all the way down onto his cock. Hissing at the contact. Feeling Rohen bare inside of me, tipped me over the edge. I crashed around him, having to use his body as balance to keep me standing up straight. He slowly slid out of me, biting my shoulder as he did it.

"Do you know how hard it was not to just fill you up when you took my cock like that."

I kissed his lips softly , making my way down the sculpted v of his hips. His hard cock was ready for me. He moaned as I took as much of him as I could in my mouth. I used my hands and worked him slowly.

"Holy fuck." He moaned and his hips bucked beneath me as he climaxed. I watched him as he came, exploding in my mouth. I wiped the corner of my mouth and started to climb out of the shower.

"Where are you going?" He asked breathlessly.

"Some of us have to get to work." I winked at him.

"You're going to be the death of me Hollie."

I finished getting ready and made my way down into the bakery's kitchen while Rohen finished upstairs. I often never cooked up there, I figured why make a mess when I am already having to clean one kitchen. I wanted a coffee and Rohen would probably want one too, this time without all the extra sugar. No blood sugar disasters were going to be caused by me this time.

I found the stevia sweetener and used the Hu salty dark chocolate I had, both had zero added sugars and the chocolate had no carbs. This time I made him an iced americano. All the caffeine but the espresso was diluted with water not milk. I was not a four am kind of breakfast person, I hope Rohen wasn't either. I sat our drinks aside and started to map out my morning. This week's display will transition to the large gingerbread houses and cookie kits we sell. They were always a hit. Plus gingerbread was one of my favorite cookies.

I moved to the pantry and drug out the 50 lb container of molasses. I had to huff and grunt to move the damn thing.

"What the hell are you doing?" He was clearly amused that I was battling this giant ass tub.

"I need to move this by the mixer. It's gingerbread day."

"Isn't that everyday for you?" He squatted and picked the tub up with ease, placing it beside my large pink stand mixer.

"No, it's not for your information."

"This is a special gingerbread day?" He looked amused.

"Oh fuck off." I shoved his shoulder.

"You're welcome, gumdrop." I handed him his iced americano, he looked at it intriguingly.

"Are you purposefully feeding me sugar to become my caretaker? Is that your fetish? Some kind of freaky Hansel and Gretel shit."

"It's sugar free and I made sure there are not a lot of carbs in it either. It shouldn't cause you to spike."

"You really did that for me?" He swirled the iced coffee cup.

"Am I not supposed to be nice to you?" I broke his gaze to shovel heaps of four into the giant stand mixer.

"I kinda liked when you pretended to hate me." he winked at me.

"I'm sure you did. Are you going to walk of shame back to your parents' place."

"First of all there's no shame here." he propped himself up against my work bench. "Are you trying to get rid of me already?"

"Unfortunately not. Just curious." I turned the mixer on, the sweet smell of molasses and ginger filled the air.

"For your information, I am going to grab us breakfast and set up the display in my window to keep in line with the rest of the square."

"I am actually shocked. Rohen Frost doing something that is in line with the status quo. How non unoriginal of you."

He chuckled. The gentleness of his smile was comforting, he looked more like the carefree teen version of himself. A creeping feeling settled in my chest as I was almost waiting for the other shoe to drop.

For Rohen to just act like this was all a huge mistake and never look back.

"Where are you going to get breakfast at four in the morning?"

"It's Saturday, the biscuit barn opens at 5 am. Plenty of time to walk of shame to get cleaned up and head back. I'm sure you will be so enthralled in the gingerbread that you barely miss me." He added a wink.

The jingle of the bells on the front door had both of our attention. *Oh fuck, it's gingerbread day..* Isla was standing in the doorway, her face giving away all of her thoughts. She was in pajamas and had her insanely large day bag packed to the brim. Her other arm clutching the shop's macbook. The shock on her face, had her mouth hanging open, literally.

"Am I interrupting something?" She could not hide the squeakiness in her voice.

"No." I shrieked at the same time Rohen responded.

"Yes." Rohens words had an almost venomous touch to them.

We answered at the same time. I shot him a dirty look. Isla walking in to find him here has caused his gray cloud to come back. We all stood there in an awkward silence. I could feel both of their eyes digging into me.

"Well, Rohen I will see you in a little bit."

"Breakfast for three it is." He gave me a small smile and walked past Isla. I could see she was about to explode with questions as soon as he left the room. The jingle of the front door signaled her attack.

"Do you want to talk about it?" I rolled my eyes and plopped the large gingerbread ball onto my work surface. I couldn't let our gossip, or lack thereof, slow down my momentum.

"Ummm, I'm not sure yet."

"He totally spent the night here, Hollie." Her eyes were bugging out of her head.

"Oh, I didn't even notice." I couldn't make eye contact with her. I knew my skin was beet red by the burning sensation on my cheeks. Her snorting chuckle made me blush even harder.

"Hollie, I don't care. Just be careful with Rohen." Her tone eased, knowing our history. She was the one to pick up the pieces when my best friend left without a trace the first time. The sinking pit in my chest churned my stomach. I couldn't go through him disappearing again, not after last night.

"I know, Isla. Trust me." She walked to the front to grab a coffee.

"Are you going to tell me what actually happened? Or just avoid my questions?" She yelled from the front. I pounded the gingerbread along the table top. Rolling it just thin enough for the perfectly shaped cookies. Isla returned with her steaming mug of coffee, her messy ben flopping over her face.

"Okay, so basically he ended up not feeling well, so I took him back to his place. We ended up coming over here and it just progressed from there."

"That is the most boring hook up story I have ever heard in my life. I think I actually lost brain cells listening to that." Her eyes rolled to the back of her head.

"Isla, I am not telling you the details of my sex life."

"SO you did hook up with him?" She gasped.

"Yes! Alright, and it was amazing."

"You fucking ho, I knew it." Her smile was the biggest I have ever seen. Who knew my love life gossip would be what cracked her grinchy exterior. I was not about to get into the details about how last night with Rohen went. Flashback of him in front of the Christmas tree caused heat to rush to my face.

"So you and Rohen are doing couple-y things now?" Her eyebrows raised at me.

"No!" I shook my head. "I don't know."

"We haven't had a long time to talk, because my sister came into the bakery at the ass crack of dawn this morning."

"It's gingerbread day! I will gladly go back to bed if you do not want any help this time. We both know the mental breakdown that was caused a few years ago." I thought back to when I tried to hold together the giant window display pieces by myself. Attempting to hot glue the pieces together that were bigger than my arms. I ended up burned and covered in icing, with a not so hot window display.

I did not want to have to tell her I knew she was right. Those were the words she lived for. Her mostly perfectionistic behavior had to stem from somewhere right? I think she got too many of those complements as a child.

"I will admit I do need help. But please, don't make it awkward."

"What's going to be awkward?" Rohens deep voice caught us both by surprise. The scream that left my throat matched Isla's. Her body leaping from the counter in fright.

"What the fuck is wrong with you two?" He looked at us like we were two hysteric heroines about to face their murderer. His eyebrows furrowed as he sat the bags down onto the counter. Maybe the screaming was a little much.

"We're not used to anyone else being in here this early. Normally if a man was in Hollie's apartment at this hour, it would be because he's the holiday slinging slasher." A smile peeked at his lips.

"Sadly, not a murderer, but I have the whole biscuit barn menu in that bag over there. Gingerbread day sounded like a lot of work."

"It is," we said in unison.

"I guess we can take a break to eat, wouldn't want to pass out and be crushed by the gingerbread house." I shuddered thinking about the time I actually was almost crushed by the house a few years ago.

"Seems only logical." He smiled at me.

"Ugh, get a room." Isla walked past us heading to the front of the shop, biscuit barn bag in hand. My stomach rumbled just thinking about it.

Chapter Thirteen

One Week Later

My muscles ached as I sank down into the depths of my bathtub. The pink tile glimmered with incandescent bubbles. A light rose scented candle burned in the corner, illuminating the pink roses beside it. After this week, this was just the me-time I needed. *BUZZ BUZZ BUZZZZZ* my phone vibrated so hard it almost flew into the tub.

ICE QUEEN: Are you ready for the cooking class in the morning? Remy is going to take over the counter while we are gone.

ME: As much as it pains me, Remy is your best business move yet.

Isla had been right about hiring an assistant. After one week with Remy in the shop I was actually going to bed at 10:00 pm. I wasn't having to run myself ragged all day trying to bake, construct Christmas magic for the town, and run to the front of the store. Remy handled the front of the house, utilizing our new smart POS system. Another thing Isla integrated. She had been right about that too. She somehow managed to connect it to my ancient vintage register so it would still ching when we made a sale.

ICE QUEEN: I knew you would see the light eventually, or die trying.

ME: I thought about it tonight and I do want to take Remy up on his offer for his friend to be the dishwasher, ONLY if we can afford it.

ICE QUEEN: We cleared 10k in the weekend alone. We can more than afford it.

The money wasn't what was important to me. Yes we needed it to survive, and our parents left us this paid off bakery. We were very lucky people. I made sure to contribute as much as I could to the town that helped make it possible.

ME: You know I don't care about that.

ICE QUEEN: You should Holls.

ME: Blah blah blah

I turned my phone off and sank deeper into the tub leaving Isla to surely brood over my lack of response. After thoroughly soaking I retreated to my bedroom, reading one of my favorite rom coms until the darkness of sleep overtook me. .

.   .

BUZZ BUZZ BUZZ my phone rang off the hook.

Incoming Call Grinch

How could he be awake this early. I slid my phone open, and mumbled a raspy good morning.

"Good Morning Gumdrop." Rohens voice was laced with sleep

"Hi." I squeaked.

"I thought you were avoiding me?" He softly chuckled.

"I was not! We were just slammed this week."

"It's okay gumdrop I was just giving you shit about it."

"What do I owe the pleasure to this early wake up call?"

"Well, I woke up and went to grab the mail from my frozen mailbox and your lights weren't on, so I needed to make sure you were okay?"

"You were worried about me?" I felt like a dumb high schooler all over again. The butterflies in my stomach doing somersaults.

"Yes, your normal 3 am wake up call must have slipped past you today." He chuckled.

"WHAT!" I Shrieked into the phone.

I ran into the bathroom looking at the alarm clock on the counter. 5:54 AM. It was right there in big bold letters.

"Thank you for waking me up, I overslept on all my alarms. I am so fucked right now!" I hung up on Rohen, hopefully he forgives me. I had to get the ovens started for the day, especially if I had to leave to go into the town's activity fest for the day. I pulled the cords, letting drapes cover all the windows. I didn't need the town seeing me in my bra running around like a chicken with my head cut off in here.

Sprinting to the kitchen my fuzzy socks had me sliding across the marble floor. I clicked each oven on, the deep humming noises signaling their awakening. Scrambling about, I struggled to pull the trays down for this morning's bake. I hadn't even noticed that Rohen had crept into the bakery, watching me flounder amongst the ovens.

He cleared his throat roughly.

I could only scream in response. Not an afraid scream, more of a hysteric stress scream.

"Do you always bake half naked?" His eyes roamed over me.

My mesh bralette hid nothing, the material of my shorts matching. FUCK. I was basically utterly naked in front of him. Not that he had not seen it before. It is just different now.

"NO! Do you always break into my bakery unannounced?" The tension oozed from his body, tinging the air with its heaviness.

"Yes, hence the breaking and entering part." His eyes shot me a wicked gleam. "Let me help."

He made his way closer to me, our bodies mere inches apart. His full lips twisted upwards in that devilish smirk. Gods how I loved that smirk. It made my heart soar. But my head warned me to keep myself guarded.

"Absoluetly the fuck not." My hands connected to the warmth of his chest. The first time I had touched him in nearly a week. Lightly shoving him back. I hushed my thoughts at how hard his chest was beneath his clothes. I don't have time to make stupid decisions today.

"What did I do?" His arms crossed his chest. His eyes devouring me beneath his gaze.

"I just do not need you in the way here, or distracting me. I am already so behind." My voice rose in octaves as my hands pointing to the racks on racks of trays that have yet to be baked.

" Well Miss Winter, tough shit." His tall frame went to the front of the store. I could hear the chairs scraping the floor. The doors clicked into place. Rohen was opening the front of my bakery while I scrambled about in the kitchen.

Two hours later and every pastry had been baked, every cupcake had been frosted. The pastries shone in their clear cases waiting to be chosen. New white marker flurried snowflakes and the daily goodies names across the case. The smell of fresh espresso shots wafted in the air. Drifting the coffee smell into every single one of my senses. The first sip was heavenly and just what I needed to help fix this shit show of a day.

Dark furrowed brows stared at me from across the bar. Irritation knitting them together. The bright screen of his phone illuminated the sharp features of his face. Beep after beep of notifications had Rohen distracted in whatever it was.

"Rohen." My voice was meak, wanting to pick up the conversation. But not really knowing how. I felt like we were in that awkward limbo stage. There was so much to figure out, well, if we were even going to figure something out. What were we doing? Is he actually staying? My mind reeled with the possibilities causing my stomach to turn. It would be easy just to slip into bliss and not pretend there was another shoe going to suddenly drop. Kicking my ass back into reality.

"Sorry, it's my firm." He mumbled softly. His lips pursed in a tight line. His fingers furiously typed away at the keyboard. Rohen had not talked about the firm much. Well, not at all since he got here. I sort of forgot that was even a part of his life since he jumped head first into his parents store. His face did look extra broody right now, so I assumed it was not good news he was hearing.

"Everything okay?" My eyes watched him while I sipped my coffee. His tall frame still stopped over the counter not budging. We still had about an hour before the bakery opened, and the customers did not need to have XXX Hollie serving them cookies today. So I left Rohen in whatever world he was in to get ready for the day.

When I came down to open the doors Rohen was gone. He left a note under his cup.

Work problems, I have some things I have to handle ASAP.

I will see you Friday night, it's a date.

I couldn't help the anxiety that crept into my chest thinking about not seeing Rohen for another week.

Chapter Fourteen

"*R*eally Hollie. You couldn't dress like a normal person for once. You had to look like that while we're teaching a cooking class." Isla had her hands on her hips circling me like a vulture.

We were teaching a cookie class this week at the town hall as part of the winter festivities. We had almost 100 people sign up. I was beyond excited to come today. Normally, I would be riddled with anxiety leaving the bakery and doing this by myself. However, the bakery is in good hands leaving me to do more fun things like this.

Isla was mad because we had our pastel pink T-shirts with our vintage santa logo on them today. But in true Hollie Fashion I had spice it up a little bit. She did not appreciate my over the top Christmas outfits. Today I had on light wash mom jeans that had a somewhat scandalous slit under my butt. But I had found some GORGEOUS heat transfers from etsy to add to them. My legs had white glittering snowflakes all over the fabric of the denim. A sheer glittering mesh top acted as sleeves for my T-shirt. I had to wear my pink platform converse to go with the pink santa vibes. I even had a pink headband with crystals, pearls, and snowflakes on it to match. It was one of my favorite outfits I had in my closet. Plus if I had worn my gingerbread overalls she probably would have murdered me.

"Isla, I can add some holiday cheer to your outfit if you need me to. Just say the word." I winked at her. She rolled her eyes and bopped the tiny snowflake attached to my earlobe.

"I am surprised this addiction hasn't has not convoluted every holiday. Who knows, next year we may see you transform into the turkey version of Hollie for Thanksgiving."

I rolled my eyes at her comments. She shoved a large bag of place cards and a chart into my hands. You set up the cookie settings while I get to work on the broadcast. For some reason that made me nervous. We were just putting ourselves onto two screens so the people in the back would be sure to see us. But, It still made me jittery. I brushed away the nerves thinking about the good this event does for our town. Each ticket is $50 to attend and we sold out at 100. Every dime goes to the community center. I can survive today knowing that we're helping so many families.

"Hollie!" Isla's sharp voice chirped. It snapped me out of my daydream. Fuck, she was mad. I didn't need her to blow a gasket today. I hurriedly began to review my chart.

FRONT

My heartbeat quickened seeing William's name. Surely Isla knew how this was going to go today if he was beside me.

UGH. I moved on to the next row.

FROST 1, FROST 2, FROST 3, LYLA....

I truly was going to die today. No matter how much Christmas cheer I poured into my outfit, it would not be enough to get me through this day. ALL the Frost's were going to be here. Which I assumed meant Rohen would be as well. He had dodged most of my calls this week. I held out hope that we would still see each other on Friday to talk about everything. I would have to watch Lyla be beside him for however long this damned thing lasts. I shivered at the thought.

After what felt like an eternity I had placed every seating card on the rows of red and white table cloths. The aisles looked like Candy Canes. Each spot held a large palette with multiple cookies, assorted pre-made royal icing bags, and all the finery for toppings. I decided to be bold and include a gingerbread house in this kit. Isla thought I was insane. But seeing it here today, made it all worth it. A separate table flanked us lined with over a hundred bags of white frosting. Ready to be used on the gingerbread construction. We had an array of candy and baubles to go on the houses as well.

Isla was setting out the free T-shirts and canvas totes with goodies when the loud door banged. William strolled in, looking effortlessly dashing as always. He had that aurora about him. That everything was always so easy to him.

"Hollie you look absolutely stunning." He said as his arms wrapped around me. I could smell his orange and cardamom scented cologne in his embrace. There was something about him that always comforted me. He was such a kind man.

"Thank you Will, you look handsome as always." His white teeth flashed at me in response and I swear he blushed. The mayor BLUSHED at me. Well today will be interesting to say the least.

"It looks great in here you two, really. Thank you so much for doing this. I know normally it is hard for you to do these things." He walked over to Isla to give her a welcoming hug.

"I can't take credit for the looks, just the organization. You know Holls. It will always look cheerful where she goes." Will-William looked at me, his eyes gleaming.

"She does that, doesn't she." Alright, what the actual fuck. I know he has had a thing for me but can I flirt with him? Rohen would be pissed, wouldn't he? I actually don't know what or how Rohen feels about this. Because we have yet to talk about whatever *this* is. But I am pretty sure in the girl code there has to be a thing about not flirting with someone else when you hooked up with your lifelong enemy-crush-friend thing. Right?

At some point in my delusional state people had started piling into the auditorium. Will made his rounds with the community members, finding Brandy in the crowd. They made their way up to the front.

"Welcome everyone!" Brandy clapped, gathering the crowd's attention. Her voice was firm, she was used to speaking to crowds at the community center. Her long salt and pepper hair was braided away from her face. Her hazel eyes lined a thin rim of coal, gold glittered shimmered around them.

She was beautiful for her age, she had the same effortlessness that her son had.

"Thank you for coming today, this event is making a direct impact on our community. With your contribution today we are going to be able to make sure the kids of Thistle grove all have paid meals for the entire year!"

The room broke out in applause. Brandy turned her gaze to Isla and I.

"Thank you to the two beautiful ladies from Hollie's Bakery, they made this possible today." She applauded, and Willam squeezed my shoulder before heading up by his mother.

"Thank you everyone for being here today. Without holding you up any longer we are going to let Miss Hollie take over." He motioned for us to take our spots at the front of the room. He let his hand brush the small of my back while we shuffled into the line. I was tense, I scanned the front few rows of the auditorium. So many smiling faces stared back at me. I noticed the Frosts were front and center, but a space was missing beside them. *Rohen.* I couldn't let my mind wander right now. I started to feel panic creeping in. How was I going to talk to ALL of these people?

Will tapped my shoulder, pretending to show me something on a sheet of paper. He had one hand firm against my back, the other grasping the paper. His voice whispered into my ear.

"Just focus on one person in the crowd. Someone you know preferably. Just focus on them, and talk to them. Sorry I am not out there for you to pick." His words made me smile. I could do this.

My eyes focused on the second table back. The little girl from the bookshop bounced in her seat. Her thick hair pulled into two ponytails on top of her head. Her little hand waved at me, her smile gleaming.

I made a small wave back, and she squealed, hitting her dad on the arm and pointing at me.

"Welcome Everyone, My name is Hollie, and I am going to show you how to decorate a cookie like a pro today. We are going to make a Holiday favorite, The vintage santa. You should have everything you need at your station. I also included a step by step sheet under your tray if you decide to get brave and go on without me." From there it just flows from me. It felt like second nature to tell the room how to navigate the tray of icing and trinkets in front of them. I stopped occasionally to help William and he made sure to look at me like I was the only sun in the solar system.

"Alright, I am going to come around and check on y'all." setting down my own piping bag. Admiring the work of neat rows on my gingerbread roof.

"Hollie, I have to steal you first. I need you to triage my cookie. It's carnage over here." William asked, his eyes gleaming at me.

"Only, because you are the mayor Will." I winked at him.

He scooted over so I could see the damage that he had done. That little girl from the bookshop could have done better. His cookie was a brown blob of icing with a melting pink swirl.

"Very Picasso-esq." I giggled at him, poking at his cookie. My laughter seemed to cause an encouraging spark in William.

"Can you help me fix it? I can't get the bag to work without flooding the cookie."

I gesture towards the piping bags and William hands me one. Williams hand closed over mine and I led him through the motions of the frosting.

"I think I will just pick up cookies from the bakery If I ever need any. This should be criminal, how bad it looks." He laughed from behind me.

I couldn't help the giggle that escaped me. I heard the *Snap! Snap! Snap!* of a camera. Jeanine from the Holiday Herald smiled at us while she snapped pictures of us in a very couple-y moments. *Great. That is what I need. For William cuddled over me on the front page of the paper.* I could worry about that later.

Excusing myself from William, we parted to head into the crowd. I bee-lined to the Frost's familiar faces. Lyla sent me a glare that didn't match the forced smile on her lips. The pair greeted me warmly, as always.

"Oh Hollie, this is absolutely wonderful! The whole setup is beyond cute!" Renee beamed at me.

"You think? I was so nervous to do this..." I trailed off my hands instinctively reaching for my hair.

"Everyone is having a blast, you should do this more." Mr. Frost chimed in. His cookies half eaten with bites out of each one.

"Too bad Rohen couldn't be here." Lyla chimed in.

"The city called and Rohen answered." Mr. Frost's voice mocked.

"He will be back for Christmas so it is all good, no stress at all." Mrs. Frost added.

"I know he has reservations at my place on Friday night, I can't wait to see him." Lylas eyes narrowed at me trying to hit me with her words. I knew it was all a game to her. It always was.

"I can't wait to see what you have on the menu now Lyla, Rohen and I are looking forward to it." I could see the muscles in her face turn sour at each of my words. Was she so delusional that he was coming there to see her.

Renee's face went from shocked at my quip to a blushing smile. Our group went silent and I decided to use that moment to my advantage. I flashed my most dazzling fake smile and headed to make the rest of the rounds around the tables. Pushing my anxiety to the back of my mind. I gathered my courage and just put on my "fake it till you make it" attitude to get through this. I had the whole great baking items, quirky outfits, and small town charm thing down. But actually seeing other humans at large gatherings was not my forte. So I just pretended for the next three hours that I was hosting my own episode of the Christmas cookie bake off.

The soles of my feet ached as I finally sat back down after everyone had left.

Chapter Fifteen

One week until Christmas

Friday was suddenly here and I was frantically getting ready. Only 15 minutes remained until I had to be ready for my date with Rohen. Oh my god. My date with Rohen. The mix of emotions was overwhelming. We hadn't talked much in the last week due to the sheer volume of work we were both doing. The picture of William and I circulating through the town's social media probably did not help. I tried to shake the mental image of his arms wrapped around me laughing. The hot sting of the curling iron brought me back to reality. *Fuck that hurt.* I sweept my curls behind my ear, slicking the front two pieces down with a wax stick. When I was satisfied with the result I checked my outfit one more time. I opted out of my traditional pink pastels and settled on a sleek black look tonight. My dark wash flare jeans hugged my figure tight. I wore a black sweater with a slanting neck line. Exposing the snowflakes on my shoulder. My kips adorned a deep red lipstick, which matched the slim sparkling rubies in my ears. With one final sweep of highlighter I figured this was the best I could do. Slipping my heeled booties on, I grabbed my purse and headed out the door.

Rohen was waiting downstairs. His eyes widened when they saw me. My favorite sly grin spread across his lips.

"Hello Gumdrop." His voice was low as his eyes scanned my body. Stopping for a brief moment on my shoulder.

"Hey Rohen." I blushed under his gaze, surely turning myself into a beet.

"I brought you something to make up for this week." he walked towards me, his hands running up my arms. He smelled divine. The touch of his fingers sent chills up my body.

"Rohen, you did not have to do that." My voice turned soft. I could not make the words any louder if I wanted to. On my counter sat a beautiful bouquet of Winter flowers. The scarlet and emerald dusted with a light coating of gold. They were stunning.

His eyes met mine and I was able to mutter a thank you to him. His finger brushed my chin, lifting my face to his for a soft gentle kiss. He wrapped his hand in mine and led us out the door. The snow was so picturesque on our walk down the street. The sidewalks had been swept clear leaving ample room to walk. Snowflakes drizzled down in a light dusting, leaving small flurries caught on our coats. The amber lights from the restaurant set the street aglow. Lyla may be a mean girl at heart but she really turned this place around.

Rohen held the door open for me, wrapping an arm around my waist once we were inside. He told the hostess our reservation time and we only had to wait a few minutes before being seated. I took notice of the dark wallpapered walls adorned with a multitude of art features adorning them. The warm wood tables were a great balance between the darkness on the walls. Bright gold chandeliers loomed throughout. An old style oil lamp sat in a glittering holly wreath on each table. Setting the features of the patrons a glow.

Once we were seated in a small booth in the back, our server brought us a plate of warmed seasoned oil and fresh bread. I took the time to settle over Rohens outfit for the night. He had worn his usual dark denim with black leather boots, but he had opted in for a black cashmere turtleneck tonight. Drawing the attention to his face, and the devious white smile.

I learned that Rohen likes his whisky neat, and he doesn't drink that often. More socially, but sparsely. I sipped on my sugar cookie martini, this was the only drink I had found that I liked.

"Do you want to share?" His eyes peered at me over the menu.

"That's fine, as long as you don't order any seafood. I am not trying to die on our first date."

"FIrst date?" His tone mocked me. It sent panic through me. This was a date right. It had to be.

"This is a date right?" I managed to stutter out.

"Yes, but I wouldn't count this as our first date." He sat the menu down to fully look at me. His full lips drawn into my favorite side smile.

"Then what was our first date?" I could feel the heat rush to my chest. I already knew exactly what he was talking about.

"The candle light night-thing. Where I found my book shrine in your library." He took a sip of his drik trying to hide his wolfish smile.

"So this would be technically our second date."

"Mhmm he purred." I hated to admit how much I liked this version of Rohen. He was always changing and as much as it gave me a headache, I loved that about him. You never knew what to expect from him.

"Hello" Our server chided. The young girl looked nervous as she rambled off the specials. Stopping to glance between the two of us.

"We will take the bacon jam appetizer with the full spread, an 8 oz filet with the house side, the Parmesan crusted chicken with the bacon brussel sprouts, and that should be good unless Holly wants to add anything."

"That sounds perfect." I nodded at the server.

"Can you make sure to add that I have a severe fish/shellfish allergy for the chef please." He smiled at the girl. Her face turned red.

" I will let him know, I think they can make the house caesar without the fish.

"I would greatly appreciate it." With that she turned and headed to the kitchen and Rohen got up and slid into the booth next to me.

"We're sharing" He smiled at me. His boyish smile made me blush again.

"We are." I laughed at him.

"How was your week, I missed you." His hand wrapped around mine. I was honestly shocked that he had missed me.

"You missed me?" It was almost like I could not believe that it was real.

"Did you not miss me? I am sure William tried to keep you company in my absence." My stomach turned at the thought of that photo.

"He tried, but he's not you is he?" His eyes sparkled at my words, clearly excited.

"No, he's not." His hand moved to squeeze my thigh. He grabbed a small piece of bread, dipping it into the warmed oil mixture. Slowly bringing it to my lips. I took it from him effortlessly, making a point to suck his fingers before he pulled away. He leaned into my ear, his breath flitting against my neck.

"Gumdrop if you do that again, we are going to have to go home." He softly kissed my ear before retreating from me.

"So with William out of the way, what else did you do this week."

"I hosted a cookie decorating class with the town. It was the most stressful thing I have ever done. But it went well and we raised a ton of money."

"I saw pictures, you looked in your element."

"Did I? Because the entire time I was trying to pretend that I was Ree on my own show to avoid a panic attack. I do not like people watching me, especially that number of people. I did see the little girl from your store in the front row. It seems she really likes me even if I am not in my Gumdrop snow fairy princess attire." Rohen laughed softly.

"Christmas is next Friday, are you going to slow down at all?"

"No, I will be busier. I am catering so many people's dinners it is insane."

"You can cook normal food too?"

" Absolutely not, unless it is toast. I make their desserts."

"Toast? Interesting." His eyes stayed on my face as I rambled on about all the things I had lined up for the week.

"How rude of me to only talk about myself, what have you been doing that took you away for a week?"

"It's not rude Holly, I could listen to you talk about yourself all day. And that is a surprise for later."

"A surprise?" I took a long sip of my martini.

"Yes, a surprise. No more questions I have no willpower and I already want to give it to you."

"Hot plates, Hot plates." Our server called as she brought out a plethora of food to the table.
Rohen made small talk with her while assuring her we were okay.Rohen had to pull out his phone to adjust

the carbs he was consuming before diving in. We spent the next hour indulging in food heaven. The new menu here was to die for. Our conversation never dulled, it seemed that we always had something to talk about. Even if he mainly wanted to focus on me. As our meal winded down he draped an arm over my shoulder. Toying with the curls that rested there.

I could hear the all too familiar *click-clack* of Lylas walk. Of course she would have to assert herself into our date. She looked beautiful, no one could deny her that. Her fiery red hair matched the red dress she wore. Her feline gazed honed in on Rohen Frost.

"Rohen I am so glad to see you here, how was everything?" Her smile was plastic and constructed to her face.

"Hollie and I really enjoyed everything tonight, thank you." He made sure to bring attention to me with his dazzling white smile. I thought Lyla was going to reach across the table and actually killed me with the look on her face.

"Oh, Hollie, I didn't see you there, as usual. Since you enjoyed such a wonderful conversation with Rohen I'm sure, did he tell you about his new project he's working on?"

I could feel his back tense. His grip tightened around me.

"Lyla, I am not sure what you're talking about."

"Oh let me see, the headline just dropped." She whipped out her phone pulling out the latest tabloid. "*Rohen Frost's literary firm releasing the next Christmas classic*. Oh! Here is another one, *Insider scoop on how Frosts firm used a relationship to gain new material*. Or! This! *Frost's firm book set to hit the shelves on Christmas Eve*! Hollie I never knew how talented your mother was. How kind of you to share it with Rohen." Her smile was sly and she knew exactly what she was doing.

My heart dropped to my stomach. There is no way he would do that. He would not do that. I stared at Lylas screen, the image of my moms book plastering the surface. I could feel the heat radiating off of Rohen.

"Lyla bill me for the tab we have to get going." His voice was menacing.

"No." I said flatly. He turned to me, his face red with anger.

"Tell me what she is talking about." I already knew in my gut it was bad, I could not shake the feeling. I thought I was going to throw up everywhere.

"Did you not understand from the headlines sweetie. He used you to get your mothers book to turn it into the next Christmas Classic to rake in money to his publishing firm." She made sure to annotate each word with venom. I could not help the hot tears that escaped my eyes. I looked at Rohen but he was on the phone, yelling at whomever at his phone that everything needs to be pulled now.

"Hollie." He looked at me and his eyes tried to plead with me. But that phone call settled it. He really did take her book. The one thing of my mothers that was solely mine. He had planned to mass publish it. I wanted to throw up, and I actually might. My hand gripped my stomach and I couldn't stop the tears from flowing.

"I..I have to go." I stuttered looking between the two of them.

"Hollie, wait, please." His voice trembled as he grabbed my arm. I shrugged my coat on and headed out the door. I was sure that Rohen was going to follow me and when he didn't I had all the answers I needed. I had been used by Rohen Frost.

Chapter Sixteen

It had been three days since I had ran through the snow down the street. Not caring who saw me as I jogged past. I was sure that my tears had melted my eyeliner down my face and I looked insane. Utterly insane. I did not tell anyone about my experience, not even Isla. I stayed to myself for the next three days. Only coming undone in my shower, turning into the happy baker the moment the doors opened.

That night I could not stop the tears that streamed down my face as I thought about Rohen. Had it all been a lie? It had all felt so real. The next few hours felt like a blur until I finally turned off the scalding shower water. I cried until there was absolutely nothing left. I checked my phone on my nightstand and I had 14 texts and 10 missed calls from Rohen. I wrapped a towel around myself and decided I was going to binge eat ice cream until I had to get up for work. Stepping out of my bathroom there was a hulking figure sitting on my bed.

"You have got to be fucking kidding me." I half yelled at him. "You have got some fucking nerve to be here Rohen." My voice cracked threatening tears.

"Hollie, please just let me explain. Please." His voice cracked in its soft tone. His face pained.

"You don't deserve it, Rohen. How could you?" My voice trailed off, tears choking me. He put his head in his hands and took a steading breath.

"That book was never meant to be published. Ever. It was only meant for you." I did not speak.

"Lyla had leaked articles into the media, and my fired assistant took a rather large sum of money from someone to get information about what I was doing. I would never hurt you, Hollie." He stood and tried to close the gap between us. I stepped back, and the hurt on his face only deepened.

"Please put some clothes on and I will show you." I couldn't make the words leave my lips.

"You don't owe me anything Hollie, but please just let me talk to you." I nodded and he left the room, heading to my living room. I couldn't stop the pain that wrapped around my chest. Seeing home was like my heart was breaking all over again. I was so stupid. I grabbed my favorite pair of candy cane silk pajamas. If I was going to break my heart again at least I would be in my favorite PJs before my mental breakdown.

Rohen had turned on all the lights in the living room. I had left the TV on my normal fireplace and Christmas music setting. He had on a red track suit that he used as loungewear. Something I had gifted him while he was in New York. While he was ripping my heart out I was sending him fucking gifts.

"Hollie, please let me explain." He patted the cushion beside him.

"Rohen, I don't know If I can." I couldn't stop the tears from slowly dripping down my cheek.

Against my better judgment I sat beside him making sure not to touch. My hands went instinctively to my stomach.

"Hollie, I.. Here. Just read it." He handed me a beautifully crafted oversized book. It looked just like my mothers. Except the pages were thicker. There was gold leaf and gilding in replace of her glitter pens. My hands shook as I flipped through each page. He had added pop ups, pull tabs, and so much glitter. My mom would have loved it.

"This is beautiful but I am not understanding why you were going to publish this."

"Hollie, it was never going to be published. It was for you. Only you."

"How am I supposed to believe that Rohen?"

"I commissioned artists to make the pages, I went over every single detail for you. This was only for you, not to mention it would be astronomically expensive to publish."

"You're not funny Rohen."

"Just keep reading Hollie."

I tried to fight the sense of security that he gave me. I was so mad at him. He deserved every ounce of anger. Was I really going to just drop everything and believe him?

"Rohen, really."

"Hollie, I can never tell you how sorry I am that this happened. Please, please believe me."

His emerald eyes edged with tears, I could see the pain written all over his face. I reached up to wipe away a tear that dripped from his face.

"This was supposed to wait until Christmas Eve, but that was spoiled." He grabbed my hand and placed a soft kiss on my palm.

"How I am supposed to know you are telling the truth."

"Turn to the last page."

In beautifully handwritten style was Hollie, will you marry me?

"I told you it was only for you Hollie. Only you." The rush of emotions almost made me heave. How was this real? Was this true? The man had not even told me he loved me yet, but made this. I searched his eyes for answers and the passion behind them gave me all I needed to know.

"No one on this earth was supposed to see this besides the artists that made it and you, Hollie. I swear on my life." In that moment everything clicked into place for me. I knew he was telling me the truth. I leaned in and slowly and ever so gently kissed him. I could feel the tears on his cheeks against mine. He pulled me into his lap so I was cuddled against him. He grabbed the book and brought it to us.

"Pull the last gold ribbon." His voice was firm but breathless. I slowly pulled the ribbon relieving the last secret of the book. A beautiful silver ring was at the end of the string. A large six sided diamond encrusted with smaller diamond peaks gleamed against the christmas lights. It mimicked a snowflake. Rohen untied it with shaky hands.

"Hollie, I know I haven't told you. But, I love you. I came back home and I do not think I could ever leave without thinking about you everyday. I know you are probably beyond mad at me still. I had to ask, I would have regretted it the rest of my life if I didn't."

I held my hand out in answer, letting him slide the ring on my finger. My hands cupped his face feeling the hint of stubble grazing his skin.

"I love you to Rohen, I always have." My lips trembled as he kissed me. This was actually happening. It wasn't a fever dream or some sleeplessness caused delusion. Rohen did love me and he tried to tell me in the most thoughtful way he knew how. We sat there for what felt like hours. Him just holding me and placing soft kisses against my forehead as he traced the shape of the ring on my finger.

"Am I forgiven?" He finally broke our silence.

"Yes, Rohen, you are more than forgiven." His lips were soft against mine.

"Can I stay here with you tonight?"

"Of course, I have to get up in..." I glanced at the clock. Oh gods. "Four hours."

"You are getting up at 2 am on Christmas eve's eve?" His head flopped back looking defeated.

"Yes, it's the day I push out all the orders for Christmas. You can sleep in, I will be fine."

"I am not going to let you suffer alone."

Chapter Seventeen

Two sleeps until Christmas

I awoke entangled to a rather sweaty Rohen. His massive frame held me tight against him. Silencing the annoying alarm on my phone I began scrolling through my outlook. I knew I had to get up and get started. Gently pulling at his finger I tried to remove myself from his grasp, but he only held me tighter. Pulling me back into him while he nuzzled my neck.

"Do we have to get up?" His sleepy voice made my stomach clench.

"No, you can stay in bed, but I have to go downstairs."

"I am going with you."

"Rohen, really sleep until it's at least normal people time, go on a run and then you can bother me all day."

"Are you sure? He kissed my ear, running his hands over my hips.

"Yes, I am positive."

"I will grab us breakfast on my way back." He mumbled, closing his eyes again, loosening his grip on me.

After I had made it downstairs the ovens roared to life. I pulled up the printed list of orders and filled the ovens with tray after tray of prepped items. An hour or so had passed when I heard Rohen come down the stairs behind me. His sleepy hair was in a dark mess on top of his head. He had no shirt on revealing the sculpted muscles of his chest, the faint ridge of each ab that led to low hanging red sweatpants he had on. I couldn't take my eyes off him. He gave me a smile that made my heart skip a beat. He reached for my hand pulling me into his embrace. My back was to his chest as he wrapped his large arms around me. He traced the ring on my finger, kissing my head each time he turned it on my finger. His other hand moved to trace small circles on my stomach.

"Have you changed your mind yet?" He mumbled into my hair.

"No, I love you Rohen." I leaned back onto him.

"I love hearing you say that." he groaned into my hair. Clearly he loved hearing that as I felt him pressing into my back. I arched back into him hearing him gasp as I did.

"I am trying to be respectful of your time Gumdrop, but if you keep doing that you're going to be sore and behind schedule today." In response I arched against him again, feeling him twitch beneath me. I had almost two hours before Isla would get here. There was more than ample time to be slightly distracted.

I turned to face Rohen, his back leaned against one of my work stations. I slowly kissed down his body until I was kneeled in front of him. He watched me curiously as I grabbed a canister off the island before I settled in front of him. I palmed his hard length through his sweats, enticing a loud groan from him. He was so large, just seeing him pressed against his sweat pants had me wet. My hands tugged down his pants and his member sprang free. He was absolutely massive, there was no way he was going to fit in my mouth. My mouth engulfed the tip of his head causing him to grip the edge of the counter turning his knuckles white.

"What are you doing to me Gumdrop."

"I am apologizing to my Fiance."

"For what?" He gasped as I slid my mouth further down onto him.

"For not listening to you the night of our fight." I reached for the canister and his eyes grew wide.

His jaw slacked as the whip cream poured onto his cock.

"For fucks sake Hollie. Are you trying to kill me."

Without a response I grabbed the base of his cock, guiding the rest of him into my mouth. Slowly sucking off the whip cream the further he went in. His hips bucked against me, shoving his cock to the back of my throat. His fingers wrapped in my hair to give him something to hold onto. My tongue swirled along hsi sensitive head lapping up the pre cum that pooled there. Rohen was panting above me, refusing to look away as I took him whole again.

"Hollie, I'm going to cum." He panted out, "I'm not going to last." This made me suck him harder, tears ran down my cheek as I took him as deep as I possibly could, almost gagging on the size of him. His hips bucked in a smooth rhythm until he stopped and pulled out of my mouth suddenly. I grabbed his balls palming them as I put him back into my throat. He came hard with a breathless moan. His hand wrapped in my hair bucking against me with each twitch of his cock. It was so much I couldn't swallow fast enough. Cum dripped out of the corners of my mouth as I gulped him down. I did not stop until he stopped sputtering into my mouth, I finally released him looking up to see his eyes blazing down on me.

He pulled me up to my feet and kissed me hard. I pulled his sweat pants up over his hips while he bucked into my hand again.

"Do you have any more time to spare this morning?" I knew what he was asking, and I really didn't. Not with the disinfecting I wanted to do now. I needed that work bench today.

"No, I need to get the rest of these orders started." He looked sad at my response. His hands cupped my ass and he picked me up kissing me deeply. I moaned into his mouth at the friction between my legs.

"How are you going to go all day, working, without me taking care of you. I can feel how wet you are through my pants Hollie." He grinded into me, causing another moan to escape my lips.

" I don't have time." I mumbled.

Ughhh he groaned into my mouth.

"I need a cold shower then I am going for a run. This isn't over Hollie." He put me down with a kiss and hurried off to start his day.

I eventually changed and scrubbed the kitchen down from our shenanigans. He gave me a quick kiss before he hustled out the door on a run. Familiar chimes signaled Isla had made it in this morning.

Chapter Eighteen

One sleep until Christmas

Morning light peered through the pink curtains in my bedroom. It was one of the first days since August that I had slept in. I could feel the soreness settling into my bones from yesterday. We had packed and delivered over 150 orders. I am pretty sure the smell of rum cake had permeated into my skin. It was Christmas Eve, one of the few days a year I take off. My muscles groaned in protest as I swung myself up to the side of the bed. This was the worst baking hangover yet.

The bed was empty, I wondered where Rohen had wandered off too. I picked up my phone. 10:11. I really did sleep in late. Thankfully we decided to power through and make all the food for today last night to take to Rohens parents house. My stomach fluttered with a newfound anxiety. It is normal to spend Christmas there since our parents died, just not with Rohen, and definitely not as an engaged couple who skipped the whole dating phase. Isla tried to explain the girl math behind a lifelong sequestered love versus dating math and how it was about the same. I still can see the shock on her face as she grabbed my hand the moment she walked through the doors yesterday.

I thought she was going to lecture me or be mad at me. I couldn't have been more wrong, she pulled me in for a bear tight hug jumping us up and down. We called Rohens parents and he told them we have some news. I am sure they could figure it out partially. I made my way to the closest to try to decide what I was going to wear today. We were going to go to the towns gathering in the square, and then stay for the rest of the night. After I fumbled around I had pulled a christmas plaid jumper with a stark white blouse with a ruffle neckline and a small ruffle detail on the sleeve. I pulled red stockings out to go with my navy platform Maryjane shoes. I found my vintage gold and pearl drop earrings to top the look off. I was honestly more excited to get dressed than I was to actually leave the house.

I laid everything out on the bed and stared at it just to make sure it was the vibes I was going for.

"Why so serious?" Rohens voice came from the doorway.

EEK! I almost jumped out of my skin. He was leaning against the doorway covered in sweat from his morning run.

"You almost scared me to death." I practically yelled at him.

"You look very much alive to me." He came over and planted a small kiss on the top of my head before ducking into the bathroom.

"Rohen, what are you going to wear today?" It sounded stupid as it left my lips. Rohen only had one red shirt that I would deem Christmas worthy. He normally dressed in his signature grim reaper black.

"I figured my Candy Cane fiance would not let me wear my normal funeral garb on Christmas eve so most likely the red sweater I bought to impress you." He called from the bathroom. I heard the water click on. Unbuttoning my pajamas I decided to join him. He paused from stepping in when he heard the door creak. His jet black hair falling over his forehead. His green eyes watched as I undid each button to free myself, I could see he was more than happy for me to join him.

Once I had kicked away the pajama pants he pulled me closer to him.

"Merry Christmas to me." He mumbled as his fingers traced down my collar bone to circle my breast. My breath hitched at his touch.

"Rohen." I breathed

"Mhmmm." he replied as he knelt before me. He was so tall his face was at my chest. He took my breast in his mouth and I couldn't cover the moan that left my mouth. His large hands traced my inner thigh until he met my heat. He teased lightly touching my slickness, before plunging a finger in.

"Is that what you needed?" He asked before returning to torture my breast.

"Yes!" I panted as I shamelessly rode his finger. He slid another in, stretching me. Causing me to gush under his touch.

"That's my girl." he said as I could feel myself squirting around him.

"Rohen, I need you."

"Anything you want." He gently slid out of me and kissed my lips gently. He turned the shower off and pulled me into the bedroom. I quickly moved my outfit and pulled him onto the bed with me. His kiss was so soft, so gentle. He parted his lips letting my tongue have access to his mouth. He tasted warm and minty. My teeth pulled at his lip causing a moan from him. His hands went to my hips and tugged me to straddle him.

"Rohen..." I trailed off.

"What's wrong?" He looked at me with concern in his eyes.

"I'm not on birth control right now. I stopped taking it a few days ago. We can stop if you want to."

"Hollie, it's your choice."

"Are you sure?"

"Hollie, I am yours." he traced the ring on my finger. With that I sank down onto his length causing the both of us to moan. I pushed down harder trying to fit every bit of him inside me. He was so deep it almost hurt.

"Fucking hell Hollie."

His hands moved to my hips and I gripped the headboard behind him. His mouth found its way to my breast again while I adjusted to him. Once I was ready I started to slide myself up and down his length.

His hands went to my waist to help guide me. He picked up the speed bouncing me onto him.

"You take it so well baby." His eyes were locked onto us as he watched himself slam into me.

"Rohen, I'm about to..." He reached out and started rubbing my clit. Causing my vision to explode with stars. I cried out loudly as I clenched around him over and over. I couldn't help the moans escaping me when I felt him pulsing inside me. He moaned with each hard thrust, pushing him deeper and deeper into me. I needed more, I gushed just thinking about it.

"Hollie." He moaned softly. I lifted myself off his still hard cock. His cum dripped out of me. I put my back to his chest and slid back down onto him. Rohen let out a shaky breath behind me.

"Do you need me to fill you up again?" He whispered into my ear. I nodded in response, unable to make the word come out of my mouth. He pulled me flush against him, his hand moving to my knees. He spread me all the way open, hooking my legs over the outside of his thigh. I moaned as it made me take him even deeper. I closed my eyes and tucked my head against his chest. One of his hands went to my breast. Making small circles around my peak. The other moved to my most sensitive spot. Drawing small lazy circles causes me to buck at the friction.

I could feel him smile into my shoulder at my response. He started moving his fingers faster, keeping the light delicate pressure against my clit. My body bucked against him, needing him deeper, if that was even possible. His breath was hot against my ear, he kissed and nibbled until it made me gush around him.

"Do you like that baby?"

"Mhmm." I nodded

"Say it, Hollie."

"I love it when you play with me."

"Do you feel how hard you make me?" His fingers picked up the pace. I clenched around him causing him to gasp.

"Do you like knowing that just feeling yourself on my cock will make me cum. I'm trying so hard not to just explode inside you again. Not until you're fucking coming again."

"God Rohen it feels so fucking good. I just want more." He switched hands, bringing his finger up to my mouth. I sucked his fingers tasting myself on them. He moaned and his fingers moved faster. I sucked his fingers harder as they pumped into my mouth. Rohen hastily grabbed my hip pinning me down on him while he circled my clit faster. I bucked and bucked my hips against it. Causing his cock to hit the back of my pussy. I screamed as we climaxed together. His cock pulsing so hard inside I could feel his come hit the back of my pussy. We laid there for what felt like forever completely spent. My legs felt limp.

"Can we stay in here the rest of the morning?" He asked me kissing my shoulder

"Rohen we have to get ready sometime.

"It's only 12. We still have three hours until we have to leave." He ground his hips with each word. How is he hard again already?

"Hollie, I need you. I can't get enough of you. You let me fill that fucking pussy up and I need to do it again."

"Rohen." I whimpered. He pulled my face to his kissing me deeply, and lovingly.

"I love you Hollie."

"I love you too, Rohen." I could feel him harden at my words. Stretching me from the inside out.

He flipped us where he was over me. His hips pinned mine into place. He leaned across to my night stand grabbing the pink box I kept in it. Blush raced over my skin. He had for sure snooped around my things. He traced the redness in my cheeks.

"No need to be embarrassed love." He opened the box beside us pulling out my assortment of toys. He pulled out three of my toys. One large dildo, a wand, and a small clit stimulator. He grabbed my pink glitter dildo and traced where we were joined. Lubing it up.

"I want you to suck my cock, but I can't let any of my cum drip out of that pussy." He pulled out, replacing his cock with the silicone one. I almost felt empty. This was nothing in comparison to him. He grabbed the purple circle, turning it on. He moved down my body spreading me with his finger. He licked at my clit. Making me gasp in response. He pulled my folds back to fully expose it. Placing the device onto my clit, making sure it was suctioned on.

I quickly got on my knees, shaking from the power of the toy. His cock was glistening with a mixture of our cum. Fuck, this was the hottest thing I had ever experienced in my life. I grabbed his balls and massaged them while I slowly took him in my mouth. I lapped at his head where he was already dripping pre cum. He gripped my hair in response. Bucking deeper into my throat. He picked up a slow rhythm as I gasped around him. He started moving frantically as I gripped him harder. I smiled around him, satisfied that I was drawing that sort of reaction from him.

"Hollie, I am about to cum." He gritted out between clenched teeth. He grabbed my hips and turned me around. Pulling out the dildo in my pussy with a pop. before I even had a chance to breathe he was inside me. Each stroke is deeper than before. He pushed the small of my back until my knees couldn't spread anymore. I was almost in a split on the bed with him behind me pumping into me. It was too tight. Too deep. The stimulation on my clit was tipping me over the edge. Rohen palmed my ass as his pumps became sporadic.

"Come for me Hollie." I was gone at his words. I felt his cock fill me and my climax exploded with a blinding hot wave. He rocked into me until he was spent.

He pulled me up to the chest as we laid back on the bed.

"I think we both need to shower now." I breathlessly laughed.

"You're going to have my cum dripping out of you all day at this rate. I don't think a shower is going to cover it."

"I can't believe we just did that."

"I think you unlocked a kink I didn't even know I had." He laughed

"I really don't think I can face a crowd of people after that. Much less walk around town all night."

"We can stay here." He traced my hair.

"Rohen, we can't."

After some kid like arguing we finally were able to shower and get ready to leave the house. Rohen seemed awfully excited to get me out of the house.

"Let's drop our bags off on the porch. I have something to show you."

"Okay?" I agreed quizzically

He grabbed my hand and we walked down the snow covered street. Just a short few minutes away we were standing in front of the old pink house on Frost lane. Rohen pulled me towards the steps.

"Rohen this is someone's house we can't just go up to the door!" I saw the for sale sign had disappeared last month. Someone had finally paid the large sum that the seller had asked for. I am surprised someone actually paid that for this house.

Rohens emerald eyes gleamed as he pulled a shining gold key from his pocket. He unblocked the old gold door knob with a loud click. Letting the door swing wide open for me. My stomach flipped as I took the initial step over the threshold. Walking into a large foyer with a dazzling chandelier. A large war wood vintage stairs case swirled and wrapped into a second story. Reflecting the light of the tiny crystals. Rohen walked in behind me, shutting the door lightly.

"Rohen, what is this?"

"Well, I planned to go all or nothing in my proposal to you. You would walk into this house and open the book and say yes, or I would move in here alone and try until you got tired of me and pity married me." His white teeth gleamed in his most dazzling smile.

"How did you even get this house?"

"When you and your fiance have talked about this house their entire lives you don't let it go when it hits the market. Plus it's a small walk to the bakery."

"Rohen, there is no way we can afford this. I did pretty well for myself at the bakery but this house was listed at almost 2 mil. After all the renovations they did." His face somewhat dropped at my words.

"I sold the firm Hollie. I sold it all. That's what I was doing in New York. I am now a silent partner. I will still have some income, but not the responsibility that I did before. I passed the torch to say."

Horror scorched my face.

"You did what!" I shoved him.

"That was not the reaction I was expecting."

"How could you do that Rohen, that was your life's work. That was your passion, your dream!"

He stepped forward grabbing my face.

"Hollie, I couldn't lose you again. This is what I want. You are what I want. I want to live in this ridiculous Christmas town with my barbie doll wife who is a baker. I want to sit across the street in Frost's and watch you read to kids. Our kids. I want to be near my parents. I promise this is what I want." I jumped and he caught my legs around his waist. I kissed him harder than I had ever kissed anyone before. If this wasn't proof that Rohen actually loved me then I didn't know what was. He kissed me back feverishly.

Once we separated I was panting for breath.

"I want to get married tomorrow" I told him while holding his face. He kissed me to confirm his answer.

"We need to get to your parents house." He put me down and I rifled through my purse for a makeup wipe. I wiped the red lipstick off his face. His face is still evident from our kissing. His lips were swollen and extra pink. Not to mention the devilish look in his eyes. I opened the powder room to touch up my lipstick again. I finished my lipstick and caught his eyes in the mirror watching me.

"No funny business at your parents house." His look soured.

"I am serious."

"You don't think we can be quiet."

"No, I don't. And I don't want your parents hearing me screaming on your cock okay."

He moved behind me, placing his arms on both sides of mine. Trapping me to the vanity.

"Are you so sure about that?" He pressed himself against my ass. Against my better judgment I ground into him. I knew we didn't have the time for this but I couldn't help myself. I heard his zipper unzip as he shuffled behind me. His hands moved to my hips lifting my jumper over my hips. Only leaving my red thong and thigh high stockings exposed.

"You are fucking kidding me right. Telling me I can't touch you but you look like this?" He leaned us forward so his head could rest against my neck. His fingers slipped under my panties. Which were soaked through with his cum.

"Just fucking kill me now." He said as he teased my entrance, feeling how wet I was. I could hear him pumping the shift of his cock behind me.

"I want to watch you in the mirror."

"You do?"

He lifted me up where my heels were on the edge of the counter. He was so tall it was the perfect height for him. He slid my panties to the side. Teasing me with the head of his cock. I looked at us in the mirror and his eyes were deadly. His emerald eyes clouded with lust. Staring at me. I had to admit, I looked pretty hot right now. Obviously Rohen thought so too. He spread my lips in the mirror.

Watching me look at myself. I could see his seed dripping out of me earlier. This position made it hard to control it.

"You are so fucking sexy Gumdrop." He rubbed his cock into the dripping wetness.

"I want you to watch yourself. Watch yourself come undone on me." He dipped the tip of his cock in and then rubbed it against my clit. Moving both his arms to hook under my knees. Fully splaying me in the mirror. I move my arm to guide him into me. Wanting to feel the stretch of him. He gently eased in ever so slowly. I watched his face in the mirror as he buried himself to the hilt. I had finally adjusted to his size. Being able to fully take all of him. He buried his face in my hair as he shuddered, fully sheathed in me. His eyes locked on mine as he slowly pulled out of my. My hand moved to circle my slit while he fucked me.

"That's it Gumdrop."

He slid back into me with a hard thrust, jolting us forward. This was pure lust, pure need. He slammed into me harder than ever before. Shaking the mirror on the wall with each trust. My fingers worked faster as I chased my climax. I watched his eyes turn darker and darker as he growled with each thrust. Claiming what was his. I arched my back trying to push him deeper as my legs started to shake. I couldn't hold on any longer. I closed my eyes.

"Open your eyes now Gumdrop." His voice was so hoarse, so full of need. The sound of our flesh hitting filled the air as he pounded harder into me. I screamed trying to grip onto something as I felt my climax rock through me. My eyes locked on the spot where he thrusted in and out of me. A few seconds later I could feel his cock busts inside me. He moaned violently as he came letting my muscles milk him dry. Once he had finally stopped cuming he slowly pulled out. Still holding me in the mirror where we could both see his cum all in my pussy. He moved one hand out from my leg and slid my panties back in place. He sat me down gently with a kiss fixing my skirt before zipping his pants back up.

I do not know what on earth I did to get a man that liked to pleasure me like Rohen did. I think a lot of it is the whole romance fantasy author thing. He knows what women want, and what sells. He is basically acting out all of my book boyfriend fantasies. He tried to straighten himself in the mirror. A mischievous smile on his lips.

"What is it Rohen."

"I just can't believe that you're going to be my wife." I smiled back at him.

"You have to stop smiling like that, everyone is going to know."

"Know what?"

"Rohen." I said flatly.

"We are two consenting adults that just got engaged and are getting married tomorrow. Excuse me if I want to make love with my super hot wife. If people knew about the whole knee high, thing thing they would understand."

"Rohen!" I yelled and smacked his arm.

"Lets go to my parents house I guess." He smiled at me.

Chapter Nineteen

One sleep until Christmas

Our bags had disappeared somewhere within the Frost residence when we made it back to the front porch. Rohen opened without knocking, christmas music and conversations filtered through. There had to be more than just his parents in there. He wrapped his hand around mine and pulled me through the doorway. It smelled heavenly here. Warm cinnamon, some kind of smoked meat, and just an assortment of dishes wafted through the air. I was so hungry I had forgotten that we had not eaten today.

"Rohen! Hollie!" Renee jumped up from the couch to hug us as we entered the living room. Their living area opened up to a large two story vintage washed brick fireplace. A giant L shaped couch surrounded it. It was filled with people, much like the rest of the house.

"Mom, you didn't tell me it was this big of a party nowadays."

"Well, thankfully you're here this year to experience it." She shoved his shoulder and pushed him aside to hug me.

"You were always a part of our family Hollie, I am just so so happy for you two." She had tears in her eyes when she pulled away from me.

"Well I am going to steal my wife to be to get me some food. Type 1 diabetic and all. I think I am crashing."

"Rohen! You're not using that as an excuse to hide away all night!" Rohen grabbed me again and hurried us into the kitchen leaving me niggling at his childishness.

"She is right, you know."

He nodded as he grabbed two plates stacking them high with food.

"I am pretty low right now. I have just been rather.. Distracted today." He shot me a smile. I will put the app on your phone whenever we sit down tonight. That way you can yell at me too. He ushered us to sit outside on the patio. The Frosts had heaters installed to still be able to enjoy the many winter months here. There were so many people here. A lot more than last year. Rohen grew quiet as he started eating, enjoying all the catering from the afternoon.

I heard the Click clack click clack of my nightmares. Damn she was everywhere. Lyla came up to our table and immediately focused on Rohen. Of course. She looked stunning as always. In her all black outfit. It was a stark contrast against her bright red hair.

"Rohen, I am so glad that you are here this year for Christmas. There are so many fun things you have been missing. I will just have to show you some of my favorites."

"I'm sorry Lyla, Hollie has me reserved for the night." he told her with a sly smile.

"Oh you two buddies can hang out later, Rohen I really want to take you out to see the real insert town name.."

"Lyla, you are incredible and as much as I would love to, I have to get ready for my wedding tomorrow." He took a big bite of food purposefully. Making him unable to reply.

"Wedding!" She laughed, "ha ha, Rohen."

"Lyla, we really have so much to do for tomorrow I don't think he's going to make it."

"Hollie, whatever joke this is, it isn't funny." I held out my ring to her and horror washed over her face.

"We have a lot to do, Lyla, the house, marriage, baby making, you know the works. " Rohen chided in.

" Rohen you are going to regret choosing her."

"Lyla, it has always been her. There was never a choice." With that she twirled on her heels and stomped off. Surely going to crash someone else's party.

"Did you really have to add the baby making in there."

"I don't think she will get the point unless I chain you to me." We both busted out laughing at the thought of it.

We spent the rest of the afternoon making our way around the house mingling and getting congratulated about our engagement. Rohen was the happiest I had seen him in a long time. His eyes had a sparkle that just made him look alive as he told everyone that he was marrying me.

Chapter Twenty

Christmas Day

*R*enee buttoned the last of the pearl buttons flowing down my back. It was funny how fast you could get a sample wedding dress and get it altered when you've baked all their kids' wedding and birthday cakes. The dress was tight against my curvy figure. The silk curved in a deep wave over my breast, hugging my body until it pooled at my feet. The back was replaced with lace delicately buttoned down to the bottom of my spine.

Isla stepped in to fix my hair. My icy white curls pinned in a romantic up-do. I did my own makeup for the day. The same super pinky blush and glossed lips I normally went for. Renee gave me a pair of Snowflake diamonds as my something new and I almost ruined my makeup opening them. Isla gave me something old and borrowed, it was a diamond snowflake hairpin from our parents wedding. She placed it within the curls on my head. My something blue was a more private item. I had on an ice blue and white set with thigh high stockings. I blushed relentlessly when Renee asked me what my something blue was. She left it blushing with an oh deer, when she saw me turn into a beet.

I looked at myself again in Renee's full length mirror. I felt pretty normal. But today, I felt beautiful. I wish my mom and dad could be here to see it. I teared up just thinking about it. Isla put her hand on my shoulder, seeming to know.

"They would be so proud of you Hollie."

"I sure hope so."

The two women hugged me tightly. Checking every inch of me before we headed out. I never realized how many friends I truly had in this town. With the mention of Renee of an impromptu wedding the entire town had come together to orchestrate the event for us. I refused multiple times. I never wanted to burden anyone else. But everyone made it more than clear that this was going to happen. We had catering, florals, a dj, the whole nine yards thanks to all the people in this town who loved us, me more so than Rohen.

"I don't know why I am so nervous." I chattered while they pinned up my train.

"That's normal dear." Renee said.

"Here, this will take the edge off."

"Oh I shouldn't."

"Hollie one shot won't hurt you."

"I know I know."

"Hollie!" Isla squeaked.

"I am not pregnant! That's not why we're getting married! I never drink and I know I will fall and bust my ass if I have a shot."

"I didn't think about that." isla remarked

"C'mon girls let's get going." We made our way downstairs into the car waiting to take us to the inn.

My stomach twisted in knots. I pictured today as just us eloping, but I could not be more thankful and happy that our friends did this for us. We pulled up to the inn. The entire porch was covered in twinkling white light Christmas Trees. The sun was starting to set as the pink and orange rays blanched the town.

Isla led me to the small garden room before the double doors that led to the garden for the inn. One of my favorite christmas songs played in a beautiful violin and cello arrangement.

"Are you ready?"

"Yes." I managed to squeak out.

The doors opened and Isla and I walked out arm in arm. Rohen stood at the end of the aisle in an all black velvet suit. He looked absolutely stunning. Talls Pines with lights mimicked an archway behind him.

The aisle was lined in simple white and red candles. Our friends that have become our family were all there.

Isla handed me off and surprisingly William was out officiant.

"Hollie, It has always you. You are my everything and I love you so damn much. I promise to always love you and put you first. I will always support you in whatever you do in this life. Thank you for sharing your life with me. I can't wait to be a part of it."

"Rohen, you have been one of the biggest surprises of my life. I love you and everything about you. I love your creativity and your thoughtfulness. I cannot wait to spend the rest of my life with you."

His hand reached out and wiped the tear from my face.

"Alright, let the couple exchange rings." Rohen grabbed the rings from his pocket and slid a beautiful diamond band onto my finger. He placed a black steel band in my hand. I slipped it onto his finger.

"Rohen, you can kiss your bride." William shouted

He pulled me in by my waist and kissed me gently yet deeply. Everyone tossed white sprinkles in the air as we walked down the aisle. Rohen picked me up halfway through grinning ear to ear.

Chapter Twenty-One

One year later

"Rohen we are okay, I promise."

"Are you sure Hollie?" He sat down on the couch beside me, placing a snack tray and a tall jug of water beside me. Eleanor cooed in my arms. Her soft sounds warmed my soul. Rohen leaned over to kiss my forehead.

"She's so beautiful." He ran his fingers over her light blonde hair. She adorned a candy jane jumper with a big red bow hiding her blonde hair. She was laid across my chest.

"It's your first Christmas not being able to be a control freak in the bakery are you surviving?"

"Honestly, no, but she makes it better." He kissed my head again.

Aside from Elanor this year has been a whirlwind. We had moved Rohens furniture and my furniture into this house. Designing our dream home together. Rohen still writes, mostly children books now. He has taken a kind to painting, designing beautiful books similar to the one he rendered of my mothers.

The bakery has exploded. My once apartment was now an office space and our new manager stayed in the bedroom for free. She was a culinary school student and her work is just beautiful. We have begun shipping our products, delivering fresh baked goods across the country. This Holiday season was our biggest yet.

Life was changing and it was oh so Bittersweet.

Hollie's Sugar Cookies

Ingredients:

2½ cups (318 grams) all-purpose flour

2 teaspoons baking powder

3/4 teaspoon fine sea salt

2 sticks (226 grams) unsalted butter, at cool

room temperature

1¼ cups (250 grams) granulated sugar, plus ¼

cup (50 grams) for rolling

1 large egg plus 1 egg yolk

1 tablespoon vanilla extract

1 tablespoon vanilla bean paste

Instructions:

1. Preheat the oven to 350°F. Line baking
    sheets with parchment paper.

2. In a medium bowl, whisk together
    your dry ingredients. The flour, baking
    powder, and salt to combine.

3. In a large bowl, use an electric mixer fitted on medium-high speed to beat the butter and 1¼ cups sugar until light and fluffy. It can take 3-4 minutes and the mixture will be pale and fluffy. Scrape down the sides and bottom of the mixing bowl. Add the egg, egg yolk, and vanillas, and beat until well combined. Slowly beat in the flour mixture.

4. Place the remaining 1/4 cup sugar on a plate or another surface to roll the cookies in. Try to make each cookie around 3 tablespoons, divide the dough into balls, then roll in sugar to coat evenly. Place the dough balls on the prepared baking sheets, spacing 2 inches apart, and flatten slightly with the bottom of a measuring cup.

5. Bake for 10 to 12 minutes, or until the cookies begin to brown. Cool for 5 minutes before removing to a wire rack to cool completely.